I Came Back from the Dead

I Came Back from the Dead

Shimon Eliezer
The S.E.G.

PARTRIDGE
A Penguin Random House Company

Contents

Contents

Factual information in this book is taken from Shimon Eliezer's Kabbalah book.

The Assassin

It was a rainy, grey January day, and the assassin was in a suburb of Chicago in an old cemetery that lay behind the barbed wire fence of the state prison. He stood in front of a tomb with the number 7328 painted on the rough stone. He couldn't take his eyes off of it, for it was he who was buried in this muddy lot.

It all had started seven days ago in the parking lot of a shopping centre. He had been looking to steal a car and had been watching for isolated prey, which he'd found in a man dressed in a pair of jeans and a green parka. The man was the perfect prey because his car was in a dark corner of the parking lot. The man was in his forties, with black hair and a noble face, a good face, meaning not a tough guy and less chance of danger for the assassin.

The victim begged for his life, offering money.

The assassin said, "Give me your wallet and car keys."

The victim complied, saying, "Please, do not kill me. Here, take everything I have. I have two young children and a wife. I will not tell the police."

The victim then handed over his mobile phone, but the assassin shot him without blinking an eye and mostly without remorse, all to steal his car and his wallet.

Killing was part of the assassin's activities as a hit man, a hired gun, but this last killing was for free, just because he needed a car. He didn't even know the man's name; the man just happened to be there. It could have been anyone else instead. The victim was in the wrong place at the wrong time.

A woman witnessed the murder and called 911 from her mobile phone. She gave detailed information about the crime, including the license plate of the stolen car.

The police gave chase to the stolen car within minutes, locating the assassin 3 miles from the scene of the murder. Three police cars came from different directions and blocked his way. He tried to escape, and the police shot at the stolen car repeatedly. He was hit in the chest and in the head. He died on the spot, and the stolen car hit the police cars and flipped over in the air, tumbling for at least 100 feet.

He regained consciousness in the morgue – at least that was what he thought at the time. He was lying on a metal table, and a man and a woman in white shirts and plastic masks were looking at him. The man was holding a scalpel and was about to cut open his chest. He screamed, "Hey! What are you doing?" He tried to grab the man's arm, but his hand went right through it. He watched the knife cut into his chest. Strangely, he did not feel a thing.

He stood up in a second and was about to shout again, but he suddenly froze. He saw himself lying on the metal table with a number of bullet wounds. "Hey! Wake up!" he screamed at his corpse. He tried again to hold the man's arm, again without success; his hand went through.

Oh, shit! Am I dead? He'd then remembered all that had transpired, and he'd understood that he was in the morgue and that the man and the woman were the coroner and his assistant. That was fresh in his memory.

Now he was buried in a grave, his name not even mentioned. All the graves were similar, just numbers on the tombstones, probably all criminals. All his life's memories went through his mind like a movie, and he could not change stations with a remote control. He had to go through all the murders he had committed. He tried to hold back the rolling images from coming to the fore, but that was impossible. He suddenly felt various invisible presences. They were probably viewing all his memories and murders, but he did not feel any remorse. Killing was in his nature; he had grown up in that kind of environment. Now his life was over, but he did not realise how serious and definitive his situation was.

"I am tired of standing here," he said aloud, but it was all in his mind. He tried to leave, but something pulled him towards the tomb. He fought to no avail. His legs began sinking in his resting place. He tried to yell, but nothing came out of his throat. He felt the ground invading his body; it was a weird and painful sensation. He was now back in his decaying body and could feel all the worms and other vermin coming out of him.

For the first time ever, fear invaded his entire being. An abyss of darkness was beneath him. "Oh, noooo! Mama, I am scared. Help me, pleeeeease, wherever you are. Maaaaaama, no, no, no!"

He was fully aware of what was happening to him. Time and space had no relevance in this dimension. Slowly his body turned to a slushy, gel-like matter that was slowly absorbed into the muddy ground. His passage into the ground was atrocious and painful. Each single moment of decomposition was an unimaginable and terrible torture which no human could withstand.

His soul did not depart from him; it was embedded in his corpse. For him, the body was everything, and he thought that when a person died, that was the end of it. In reality the soul and the body were made of different kind of energies that were recycled after death. Now his mind became totally aware of his present condition only, forgetting his past life. He was suffering hell. Was this really the hell that had been referred to so many times during his life?

His body liquefied into a dark puddle, slowly infiltrating the ground. Deeper below, other fluids joined together and flowed slowly towards the entrails of the earth – the magma. After thousands of years these dark-gold liquids would become "energy." This was inferno, where all the damned souls (that were all energies) screamed and were tortured and kept for eternity until they were burned and consumed.

The Victim

I was standing in a cemetery, looking at a tombstone engraved with my name: "Here lies David Hirsh." I remembered what had happened a week before.

I had been in my car, on the way to buy a present for my daughter, Lilly, for her fourth birthday. I was crazy about this little girl; she was my adorable princess. My son, Eric, was seven years old and quite a character. He was always jealous of Lilly because she received so much of my attention.

That fatal day in the parking lot of Toys "R" Us, I opened my car door and felt cold, hard metal against the back of my head. I turned suddenly and saw a scary man, a bold white man with eyes that gave me the chills.
He said in a cold, harsh voice, "Give me the car keys, and your wallet!"

I gave them to him. "Please, sir," I said, "do not shoot. I have two children—" Before I could finish speaking, I felt a burning sensation in my chest, and everything turned dark.

I heard people shouting, "Call an ambulance; call the police!"

I was rushed to a hospital. The last thing I heard was "Sir, sir, stay with us."

Since I did not have my wallet, they did not know who I was and wrote "John Doe" on the medical form.

The police tracked down who I was from my license plate number, given to them by the lady who had witnessed the shooting, and they called my wife.

4

I felt as if i were on a cloud. I could see from above all the surgeons working on me, nurses bringing surgical tools to the doctor, and others drying sweat from the surgeon's forehead.

"Hurry! We're losing him!" the anaesthetist shouted.

For a second, I was back in my body as one of the doctors applied electric shocks to my chest. After a few shocks, the electrocardiogram machine flatlined in a continuous beep.

The surgeon said, "He's gone. Stop everything; we have tried the maximum. Time of death: 10.54, Sunday, the twelfth of March, 2009."

"No! It's not possible. I'm here!" I screamed from the depth of my guts. I tried to grab the surgeon, but for some reason, my hands went through his arm.

One of the nurses said, "His wife and children are waiting outside, Doctor."

"I will tell her," the surgeon said. "This is the part of my profession I despise the most."

He went out the door, but I was there before him. There was Sarah, my beloved wife. Her face was the thing I cherished the most. Tears flowed freely from her beautiful almond-shaped green eyes and down her pale face as she bit her lovely lips in worry. She was everything I wished for in a woman; here she was, waiting to get news of the results of the surgery, twisting her hands. I went to hug and kiss her, but she couldn't see or hear me. The children were frightened and crying.

"Hi, my love. It's me. Don't worry; I will be all right," I said. My arms went through her.

"Doctor, how is my husband?" Sarah asked in a feverish and trembling voice.

For a moment, I thought she was looking at me, but behind me, the surgeon was coming, and his face was grave. She was seeing through me. It was a very weird sensation.

The surgeon said, "Mrs Hirsh, we have tried everything, but the heart was very damaged and—"

Sarah didn't wait for him to finish. "No, no, nooooo! David! Noooo, it can't be, my husband ..."

The children held Sarah very tight and cried with no sign of consolation in view. "Daddy, Daddy," my boy cried, and my little girl cried, "Mommy, where is Daddy? I want Daddy!"

I couldn't help it, and I cried like a child. "I am here! I am here! You must see me; I am here. I love you, my babies."

At that moment Sarah's dad and mom arrived. They were dumbfounded. Crying, they hugged the children. My in-laws were good people, and they loved me like a son. My parents were overseas and did not know what had transpired.

My father-in-law said, "But how? Why? Where? I cannot believe it. We have to call David's parents and brothers."

Sarah, sobbing in her desperation, did not answer. She covered her beautiful face, flooded with tears, with her hands. She did not understand the enormity of the situation. She kept repeating my name. "David, David, my love, where are you? You are not dead; you can't leave me! The children need you. It's Lilly's birthday, remember? You promised her a present."

My in-laws were devastated and didn't know how to calm their daughter and the children. It seemed that the whole world had fallen on their heads. Sarah fainted and fell, like an inanimate object. Her father and a passing nurse caught her before she hit the floor. The nurse took care of Sarah and reanimated her while her mother brought her a cup of water. I was there, and I couldn't do anything to ease the suffering of my loved ones, the sorrow that my death caused them.

Sarah demanded to see my body, and the surgeon granted her request. Sarah left the children with her mother and followed the doctor, her father holding her tightly with his left arm around her shoulders. Once inside the operating room where my body was covered with a white sheet, Sarah's beautiful face flooded with tears again, and her body began shaking uncontrollably.

The doctor asked, "Are you ready, madam?"

Her father asked, "Are you sure you want to go through with this?"

Feverishly she said, "Yes, yes."

The doctor uncovered the white sheet over my face. Oh G-d, I was so pale. Death was written on my face, My G-d, that was what was left of me? What was I going to do? Would I be like this for eternity? a shadow of my former self?"

At that moment of inattention, I heard a terrifying scream. I turned around, and Sarah had again fainted, falling limply into her father's arms that held her strongly. The doctor was ready with salts and made her smell them.

She opened her eyes and clung to her father in desperation, saying, "Help me, Dad. I need to see him. I want to touch him for the last time."

I was overcome with a strong sadness and a deep sense of impotency, not being able to ease my beloved Sarah's pain, but I also realised her love for me.

Her father helped her up, and she approached the table where I was. Her hands shaking, she caressed my hair, kissed my lips, and broke down in tears of desperation. "My love, why did you leave me? How can I live without you? My life has ended. Please come

7

back. Our children need you. I need you." She lay her face on top of my chest. She was crying, impossible to appease.

Her father tried to pull her from me, but she held on to my body. He said tenderly, "Come on, darling. The kids are scared and confused. They need you now! Come on. There is nothing you can do for him. Please be strong for them." She let go of me.

I was so devastated. What was going to happen to them? To me? Why, G-d, was this happening to us? Was this the end of me? I had so many questions and no answers.

I followed Sarah out of the operating room. She turned her head to have a last glimpse of my corpse. Mechanically, I put my arm around her waist, but my arm went through. I had to realise that I was a ghost.

My children, with their beautiful little faces that I loved so much, were scared. They didn't know how to behave or what to say.

Lilly asked, "Mommy, is Daddy coming back with us?"

Eric said, "No, Daddy is in heaven."

My little Lilly said, "No, it's not true. Daddy is here; I can see him, and he is dressed in white. Right here."

We were all frozen. She ran towards me and went through. "Daddy, you're funny," she said. "Why did you move?" She was actually talking to me.

Sarah said, "Lilly, what are you doing? Daddy isn't here; he is above watching over us. Come; let us go." Her face flooded with tears.

"You are wrong, Mommy; Dad is here. Look!" she said, looking and pointing her finger straight at me. "Dad, tell her."

I couldn't believe she could see me. She had always been very connected to me spiritually. She could feel when I was a little sad or worried. She used to come and hug me to make me feel better. Now she was here in front of me, talking to me even though I was dead.

"Can you hear me, little princess?" I asked.

"Yes, Daddy, I can hear you well. Why is Mommy saying you are away?"

"Oh my G-d, it's impossible. Can you really hear me?"

"Why are you all playing?" Lilly asked. "Is this a new game?"

Her granddad picked her up and said, "Baby, we're not playing a game. Come; we are going home. Your daddy is tired and sleeping. We have to go home."

"But, but …" Lilly began crying. "Come with us, Daddy! Come! I love you."

"Don't worry; I will come home to tuck you in, as usual," I said. I could not believe that she was really seeing me and talking to me. I thanked G-d that I could communicate with her.

Sarah whispered in her father's ear, "I'm worried. She thinks that she is seeing and talking to her father."

Her father, who was the head of the psychology department of the Mount Sinai Hospital, whispered back, "You have to understand that she is in emotional shock. She was very close to her daddy. She wants to see him so much that she is hallucinating. She believes what she is saying. It's like when children create an invisible friend."

They finally left the hospital. I followed them, going through the door without opening it. Unconsciously, I said, "Cool." From the hospital's door, I instantly entered our home, as if there were no distance in between. I realised that time and space had no effect in this dimension; I could travel instantly.

After a short while, my family arrived home. Lilly's eyes opened wide when she saw me. I motioned to her not to say anything. She took this as a game and smiled mischievously.

Eric asked, "Why are you so happy? Do you not love Daddy? Are you happy that he is gone?"

Lilly said, "No, silly, we are playing a game." She pointed in my direction.

"I don't see anything. Stop telling lies," he said.

Sarah sat down on the living room sofa. Pain and tears were painted all over her face, and her shoulders drooped in despair.

No one else had an appetite, but Lilly, all smiles, said, "I'm hungry. I want waffles."

Sarah's mother took the children to the kitchen to prepare them some food. Sarah was concerned and said quietly to her father, "I'm worried about Lilly. She is smiling and playing as if she is with her Dad. I've never seen her like this before."

"Darling, we've been through a lot today, and she is only four years old. Tomorrow she will start asking questions. Now you should call David's parents and brothers."

"Please, Dad, you do it. I won't be able to speak and won't know what to say." She cried more than before, covering her face with her pale and delicate hands.

Her mother returned from the kitchen and said, "They're eating."

Sarah said, "Dad, Mom, I have something to reveal to you two that no one knows yet. I was about to tell David this morning, but then he left to buy the presents. I'm pregnant!"

I couldn't believe my ears. Her parents were all ears, their eyes wide open.

Sarah cried even harder. "The child will never see its father." She broke down in a hysteric cry.

I was dumbfounded. I was going to be a father again, but I would not get to hold my child. "G-d, why? Why me? Why now?" I yelled, looking towards heaven. "What kind of injustice is this?"

Lilly came running, her worried little face looking at me. "What's wrong, Daddy? Why are you crying? Did I do something wrong?"

"No, my love, I just bit my tongue," I said, gesturing for her not to continue talking.

She smiled and winked at me. Everyone was looking at her, not understanding what was going on. Sarah was now completely drowned in tears from seeing what was happening to Lilly without a reasonable explanation. Her mother tried to appease her sorrow, and her father said, "I'm calling David's family to tell them what is happening here."

He left the room to make the call. My father answered, and Dan said, "Hi, this is Dan. How are you?"

My father replied, "So-so. My wife has not been feeling well lately. And you and your lovely wife?"

"Jacob, I'm here at Sarah's house, and I have something to tell you. Your son had an accident."

"What happened? Is it bad? Where is he now?"

Dan did not have the courage to tell him, preferring to delay the very sad news. "I don't want to scare you, but yes, it is serious. I suggest you take the next flight out here and notify your other children. He is at the hospital. Come soon, and be careful with your wife please. We are with him. Please hurry. Bye." He hung up before my father could say another word. His eyes were bloodshot, and he was so choked up he couldn't have said one more word if he'd tried.

When he returned to the living room, Sarah asked, "How did he take it? What did he say?"

"I couldn't tell him. I just said that David had a very bad accident. If I had told him, I think it would have killed him on the spot. It would kill me if I were in his place. This way he has time to prepare for the worst; it will attenuate the big sorrow of losing a son. A child dying before his or her parents is the worst."

Sarah was exhausted. She was holding Eric at her side and called Lilly to come to her. I told Lilly to go and not say anything. She complied without a word. Sarah hugged both of them, kissing their childish faces and tears that hadn't stopped. Sarah fell asleep sitting on the sofa with her head resting on Eric's. Eric had also fallen asleep. Lilly looked at me, wondering what all this was about.

Sarah's parents took the children to their rooms. Lilly looked at me, and I said, "I am coming with you, my princess; don't worry." She gave me a little smile and followed her grandma. After the children were tucked into their respective beds and rooms, I went and kissed Eric first and then went to see Lilly. Her eyes were heavy and slowly closing from sleep.

When she saw me, she said, "You kept your promise; you came to tuck me in!"

"Of course, baby. Can I talk to you as a grown-up?"

"Yes, Daddy."

"Listen, princess, I will probably be going on a long trip, but I will always be with you. When you feel sad or you do not feel good, think about me, and I will be with you in here." I touched her little head with my finger. "And I will always be here also." I pointed to her heart. "But do not tell anyone. It will be our little secret, OK? You promise?"

"Yes, Daddy," she said, her eyelids closing.

I kissed her forehead; my heart was in terrible pain. My children were my life. How could I lose them, my wife, and my family? We do not understand what treasures we have until we lose them, and then we see the true value of the things that we take for granted. We place too much value on material, superficial things.

I left Lilly's room and went back to Eric's. A real little man, my boy. I knew that he would take care of his mom and sister. He had always been protective. He'd tried all the time to prove it to me. He was smart, and I was very proud of him. I didn't think that I'd told him that enough times. I could see some of myself in him. I was going to miss him, my little man.

I then went to the living room, where Sarah was sleeping. Her mother had covered her with a tiny blanket. Sarah was a beautiful woman. She was svelte with beautiful deep-green eyes and blonde hair. Her nose was small and perfectly balanced with her pale and gorgeous face. She was 5' 9" and 56 kilos, very well proportioned.

I remembered the first time I'd seen her, a Saturday at the temple. I hadn't been able to take my eyes off her. Our first date had lasted for more than twenty-four hours. We'd known right away that we were made for each other, and that had been the beginning of a love story. A year later we had gotten married. We had been married for nine years and had loved each other without boundaries. We'd never had fights or big arguments. I would have done anything for her, and she would have done the same. We'd had too much bliss that all had ended so fast.

I was worried about this situation. How would she manage? *Why G-d?* I thought. *What wrong have I done to be punished in such*

13

an irreversible way? Please, my Lord, let this be a nightmare, and wake me up!

My in-laws were sleeping in the living room armchairs. They were good people. They loved us, and we had mutual respect and appreciation for each other. They were also on very good terms with my parents and two brothers, whom I now thought of. How would they overcome this tragedy? I was worried most for my mother, who had been having health trouble lately. I did not know what the consequences of my passing would be. How strange it was for me to say that I was dead.

I suddenly felt the need to go to see my body. It sufficed to think it, and I was in the morgue at the hospital, staring down at myself lying on a cold metal table. My face was a livid blue. This was what was left of the person I had been just a few hours ago – a father, a son, a husband, a brother. I had been a very active man, always working and developing new businesses. It had been so important to me to build an empire. I had not been rich, just in a good financial situation.

Now here, the money had no relevance. It was worthless. I wished now that I had spent more time with my little family. Sarah was expecting a new baby, my baby, that I would never know. I felt tired. Instinctively, I lay on my physical body to rest from the long and nightmarish day. Deep inside I was hoping this was just a bad dream. I prayed I would wake up from this nightmare.

A hard and metallic sound made me jump. I was about to call out for Sarah, but to my very deep sorrow, I realised I was really dead. I choked, Sarah's name staying in my throat. My new situation was this terrifying reality. The uncertainty of what was next kept me in anguish and despair.

The medical staff had brought in another victim. Oh my G-d, she was so young. Two doctors stood next to her. One doctor said, "This is terrible. Only thirteen years old. A drug overdose."

The other doctor replied, "They should sentence drug dealers to death for selling this poison to minors. We have to find who she is and tell her family this terrible news."

The first doctor said, "It won't be me."

The doctors left, and the young girl's ethereal form slowly rose from her body. She saw me and tried to cover her nakedness, not understanding what was going on. Then she saw her body. The scream was hair-raising. Three long cuts had been sawed into her body, two on either side from her shoulders to the centre of her thorax and a longer one from her thorax down to the lower part of her belly.

Her cries made me shiver, and for a moment I forgot my death and personal sorrow. "Please do not cry. I am with you. What happened? What is your name? My name is David."

She answered feverishly, "Nancy. Where are we?"

"We are in the morgue of the hospital. We have passed away and are waiting for our families to bury us. They still have to find your family. They do not know who you are or how to find and notify your family."

"I can't be dead. I was in school just a moment ago, and no, it must be a nightmare." Nancy cried hysterically, "No! No! No!"

"Please, Nancy, do not cry. There is nothing we can do now. Let us wait for our families. I have two young children, and they are also crying, because I am dead. You see what drugs do to you? They just killed you. You are so young; it is such a shame."

"But I took drugs only twice. Some of my friends told me that it was the best quality. They didn't have any problems."

"Yes, but not everyone is built the same way. We are all different. But why take drugs? What is wrong with the youth today?"

Nancy was crying so hard she probably had not heard my last sentence. I approached her and tried to comfort her. She was just a scared child, the poor darling. I was myself scared, and I was an adult. Who would take care of my children? Would they be tempted to use drugs? For a moment I shivered at just the idea that this could happen to one of my children. For me it was too late to intervene in their adult lives. Even if I warned Lilly, she was too young to understand.

Nancy started to leave, and I said, "Listen, if you want to go to your home, just think of it, and you will be there in the blink of an eye." She suddenly disappeared, and I guessed she had succeeded. I was glad to have helped a little.

I went back to my home. Everyone was up. Sarah was weak, and her mother was trying to convince her to have breakfast. My in-laws were organising all the necessary arrangements for the funeral. They were now all awaiting the arrival of my parents and brothers.

I went into the kitchen, where Eric and Lilly were having breakfast. Lilly opened her eyes wide and was about to say, "Daddy," but I motioned her not to say anything. She had a smile painted on her lovely childish face.

Since no one else could hear me, I said, "Princess, I will talk, and you just listen."

She nodded. Oh G-d, what consolation that I at least could communicate with her.

"My darling, very soon your grandparents and my brothers will be here. You are going to hear a lot of things concerning me. You know I had an accident. You are the only one that can see me." She smiled, and I continued, "It is very important to keep this secret between us."

She nodded, clearly listening carefully like a grown-up.

"When you don't see me anymore, it will mean that I'm going on a long voyage, but I will be back as soon as I can. As I told you before, anytime you feel sad or not well, close your eyes and think hard of me, and you will see me. If you can't, try harder, because I might be too far. OK, princess?"

She nodded again, and I gently kissed her forehead. She closed her beautiful green eyes. I also tried to kiss Eric, but he couldn't notice. Suddenly there were various rings at the front door. I went to the entrance as Dan opened the door. It was my parents and brothers and their respective wives. Emotions were high.

Dan embraced each of them and said, "Please, let's all get inside. We are blocking the staircase."

Sarah came in, and she couldn't help but break out in hysterical tears. She fell into my mother's arms.

My mother asked, "What happened? How is David? Where is he? Tell me the truth."

All were listening. Sarah couldn't talk. My in-laws invited them to take a sit.

Dan said, "Please let me explain." He explained what had happened, step by step, slowly and tactfully getting to my death. My parents and brothers were quiet, wearing expressions asking, "How?" They knew already that something horrible had happened.

When Dan finally said it, all my family broke into tears. There was a sudden noise as my mother fell from the sofa to the floor. My father ran to the phone and called a doctor. One of my brothers got her a cup of water, and the other made her smell perfume. Sarah was frozen, like a statue of salt. She couldn't talk or cry. She was disconnected from this reality. I looked at all of them, seeing the pain and sorrow on their faces. My children were scared and stood on the side of the living room, near the piano. My brothers went over and hugged them.

A ring at the door announced the doctor's arrival.

The doctor said, "Please, you should all go to the other room to give her space so she can breathe." He began checking my mother. After a while he said, "She had a small tachycardia. We have to take her to a hospital." He picked up his mobile phone, dialled, and requested an ambulance. He continued, "She needs rest and no strong emotions." My father explained what had happened and the reason for the emotions of the day.

In a way this occurrence reduced the emotions about my death, but everyone's eyes were still red from crying. My father seamed totally broken, unable to say or do anything. Sarah came to him, hugged him, and kissed his cheek. My father held her in his arms and said, "Cry; let yourself go. I am so sorry, Sarah, my darling. I know it's hard what is happening to all of us, and I know how much you loved and relied on David. I am sure that in this moment he is watching over us."

He did not know how right he was. I was close to them and wished that I could kiss them.

Someone knocked at the door, and Eric answered it. It was the EMTs. They came in, put an oxygen mask on my mother, put an IV in her arm, and lifted her to the ambulance bed. The doctor gave his diagnosis and recommendations.

One of my sisters-in-law stayed home with Eric and Lilly, but everyone else followed the ambulance, heading to the Mount Sinai Hospital, the same hospital I was in. I was concerned about my mother's fragile health, and with a thought I was at the hospital with her. I was the first one in place, and my family all arrived a while later.

My mother was rushed to the emergency room; my father was next to her, trying to calm her down.

"But we have to see David, for a last time?" she said with a trembling voice and all in tears.

My father said, "Please, my love, I need you in good health. I will not be able to survive if I lose you too. G-d only knows why all this is happening. He gave us our son, and he decided to take him back. David will always be within us." He said these words mostly to calm my mother, not sounding completely convinced himself.

To my sorrow I could hear and see my loved ones suffering because of me but could not ease their pain.

A doctor came in, took my mother's medical chart, and said, "Good morning, I'm Dr Goodman. What seems to be the problem?"

My father explained all that had transpired while the doctor checked my mother's blood pressure, heartbeat, and so on. He ordered all kinds of test and gave her an injection, explaining, "The injection will help her sleep for a few hours. This will ease her stress. She has to rest."

My mother slowly drifted asleep. Seeing she was asleep, my father went to update everyone who was waiting outside the room. "She fell asleep. She is traumatised. Can we go now and see David?" he said with a sad voice and slumped shoulders. He looked tired and older by ten years.

Dan asked, "Are you sure you want to go through that?"

"Yes, I need to; I have to. David was my firstborn. He was my pride, a good son, always very attentive to all our needs. He always called us at least twice a day."

Dan said, "Let's go. Sarah, you can wait here, just in case Esther wakes up."

Sarah said, "No, I will go too. I want to see him again."

19

My father said, "There is no need for either of you to go through that again. I will go with my sons, so they can say a last goodbye to their brother. Please, my daughter, listen to an old man."

She finally accepted and stayed behind with her parents, watching over my mother.

I followed my father and brothers to the morgue. The technician opened one drawer of many in the wall. There I was, lying in the refrigerated drawer bed. I looked really frozen and quite bad. My nostrils were filled with cotton. Strong shakes overtook my father's entire body. He covered his mouth with a shaking hand to avoid screaming from the pain of so much sorrow. His eyes were full of tears, blurring his sight. He could not stand up on his own. One of my brothers held him up while the other brought over a nearby stool for him to sit. They both cried too.

My father made a move to stand up and come to my corpse. My brothers helped him. He wore a yarmulke, and he and my brothers recited the prayer for the dead. *"Shema Yisrael Adonai Eloheinu Adonai Echad."* Then my father fell on my body and cried loudly, "David, David, oh, my son, oh G-d, take me but leave him so he can be with his children and wife. Please take me."

My brothers had to physically pull him away to make him release his hold on my body. I was so hurt and feeling devastated. All this was because of me, but what could I do to appease my loved ones? I was helpless and sad.

I followed my father and brothers back to outside my mother's room. All looked sad and resolved.

My father said, "We have to go and make the arrangements for the funeral and all the legal paperwork."

Dan and my brothers went with him, and Sarah and her mother stayed at the hospital watching over my sedated mother.

The Burial

My father and Dan made arrangements for my burial to be carried out that same day. According to Jewish law a deceased had to be buried the same day of his death in most cases or the next day at latest. They also hired a funerary home according to Jewish law.

They arrived back at the hospital three hours later. My mother had woken up. Dr Goodman signed a discharge to let her go so she could prepare for the burial. He didn't think she should attend the burial, but he understood that it was a must to say a last goodbye to her departed son. He gave her strong pills to keep her blood pressure down and help her stay calm. She was going to experience very strong emotional stress.

My father and Dan rushed everyone to leave and go home, so they could all prepare to go to the cemetery. I was about to follow them, but for some reason I was attracted towards the morgue. This was a new situation and feeling, but soon enough I knew why.

The drawer I was in was opened, and four older religious men took my body and placed it on a metal table. They were the Chevra Kadisha. They uncovered my body and checked it for any irregularities, like tattoos, but there were none. If there had been any, they would have been eliminated by cutting the skin of the tattoo.

One of the old men trimmed my fingernails and toenails. Another cut and removed my stitches from surgery, and one removed the cotton that had put in my nostrils the day before. Once they had completed the meticulous check of my entire body and all four had approved that everything was in conformity with the religious ritual, they washed my body completely, with a lot of respect for the deceased. One of the elders recited the Psalms of David while the others completed the necessary rituals for the dead.

All this I watched as an external viewer. This was the first time that I had assisted with such a ritual, mostly by being the dead person.

The reason for this ceremony is that we come naked to the world and must leave naked. We cannot take anything material from this world, and the body is compared to a borrowed suit that we have to return without stains (tattoos) or anything else.

Once the ritual was finished, they covered my body with a clean white sheet which would stay on until the burial, when the sheet would be replaced with my prayer shawl, supplied by my family.

At home, they were getting ready for the funeral. Dan ordered a catering service for the evening after the funeral as customary. Sarah and my parents dressed in simple and humble clothing, reflecting their mood and mourning. The rabbi called to say everything was ready at the funerary. They were waiting for us. All my friends and relatives would be arriving to pay a last respect to me and my family.

I then returned to the hospital and got into a van with the rabbi, and four men of the Chevra Kadisha, and my body was in the middle, covered with a prayer shall. We went to the funerary, where my body would rest in a simple coffin made of untreated pinewood.

Any Jewish person, rich or poor, that passes away outside the land of Israel is kept in a coffin like this one. At this point everyone is the same; no riches can be shown. No one can take anything material to the other world. You came naked, and you leave naked.

Two hours later, my family had arrived, and many more cars were still arriving. There were more than 200 people, young and old – friends, cousins, colleagues, neighbours, friends of friends, community members, rabbis, and so on. The people who attend the funeral are the only thing that shows the deceased's status and if the deceased was liked.

I stood next to the coffin, where a few at a time recited psalms. Everyone else was silent. People passed by the coffin and embraced or warmly shook hands with my family, giving their condolences respectfully. Some cried and were choked up, not able to utter a word. All these people coming to pay me respect gave me a warm feeling. Some I did not even know.

I was distracted by something. It was my sweet princess, waving her hand to capture my attention. Oh, how much I loved this beautiful face. I waved back at her and approached. She was holding Sarah's hand. She tried to run towards me, but Sarah held her firm. Sarah was so pale and beautiful. She wore no make-up and was dressed in a black skirt and a grey blouse. She looked down, unable to face the crowd. Her green eyes were red from so much crying. She had no more tears to shed.

My parents, my brothers, and her parents were sitting against a wall at the back of the hall, where the coffin stood in the centre on top of folding wooden legs. The line of people passing to pay their respects was very long. People recited the psalms in very sad tones.

I touched my little Lilly and caressed her hair. She said in a joyful way, "Daddy!"

Sarah looked at Lilly and squeezed her hand. "What about Daddy?" Sarah asked, showing a bit of worry.

Lilly said what I had whispered in her ear what to say, in order not to worry her mother to say. "I just said Daddy because I miss him."

Sarah said, "I am sorry, baby. I am a bit nervous with all that is happening. Your father is watching over us. He is in heaven."

23

Lilly looked at me and winked. I gave her a kiss on her head and said, "I love you, my baby."

She answered, "I love you too." Sarah wasn't paying attention and didn't notice.

At 5 p.m., the head rabbi called for attention and said, "It's time to go to the cemetery. Please follow the funerary van. The first car will carry the direct family and the rest can follow behind. Four police motorcycles will lead and close the line of cars and will control the traffic around us. Please let us go."

My brothers, my father, and my father-in-law carried my coffin to the van. Emotions ran high, especially for my mother and Sarah, who were in tears. My mother was heavily sedated, and my sisters-in-law held her tight to enable her to walk. Sarah held Eric's and Lilly's hands. Lilly looked all around to locate me. She finally saw me next to my father. My male relatives laid the coffin in the van. The Chevra Kadisha got also in the van and continued reciting psalms. The doors closed behind them.

All those present rushed to their respective cars. My brothers and cousins drove the first cars that contained my family. The line of cars was very long, probably forty to fifty cars. The two police motorcycles stopped traffic and led the procession into the street.

It was impressive and imposing to see this long funeral line accompanying me on my last voyage. I rode in the van because I did not know where we were going. All that had transpired the last two days was so strange and unreal. I was a spectator to my demise and to so many people's emotions. I was very confused. In a way, this funeral looked like the close of my life parenthesis, which had been quite brief.

We finally arrived at the cemetery, and everyone looked for parking spaces. The entire crowd gathered around the mortuary van. Here again, my brothers, my father, and my father-in-law picked up the coffin and followed the Chevra Kadisha.

The latter continued reciting the psalms, this time louder, and some of the crowd followed suit.

We arrived at the open grave. All gathered around the grave with my family making up the first line. I felt a pinch in my heart. The crying and lamentations grew louder and more pressing. Using two ropes around the coffin, four men slowly lowered my coffin into the open grave, accompanied by loud cries and prayers.

My parents and Sarah could barely stand, and they held each other. Eric cried too, covering his face. I remembered the day he was born and how happy I had been. I reviewed all the happy moments with him. After that I looked at my baby girl, Lilly. She also cried, not because of me, but due to seeing her brother and mother and other people crying. She lifted her beautiful, wet blue eyes to me. She seemed to be asking, "What is this all about? Why are they crying?" I came and kneeled in front of her.

Holding her baby face that I adored, I whispered in her ear, as if they could hear me, "Listen, princess, they cannot see me; you are the only one that can. This is because you love me so much. As I told you, I am going away on a long trip very soon, and since they cannot see me, they cry."

Lilly said, "So it means they don't love you as much as I do?"

"No, my darling, they love me very much, but you are very special, and you know how to play this game."

"Can we teach Eric the game so he can play with us?"

I smiled. "No, princess. It's late now, and very soon I will have to go."

"Will you tuck me in tonight?"

"If I am not gone, I promise that I will, my darling."

25

With all the emotions and commotion, no one paid attention to Lilly having a conversation by herself.

One of the elder religious men put some dirt from the ground inside the coffin atop my corpse. The only other thing inside the coffin was my *talit* (prayer shawl). My wife had given them the shawl at the funerary, and it now covered my body.

My direct male relatives, except my son, who was too young, recited the Kaddish, a prayer for the dead. My brothers and father uttered the words with broken voices, and all present answered, "Amen."

Sarah was the first one to throw a shovel of dirt inside the grave and said, crying, "My love, my life ended the day you were taken from me, from us. But I promise that you will be in our hearts for eternity. My dear husband ..." Her voice broke, and she couldn't continue talking.

I cried from the depths of my soul, but no tears came out. Eric followed suit, filling the shovel with dirt and dropping it on top of the coffin. He behaved like a little man. He did not want people to see him crying. Then it was my father's turn, and all the rest followed suit. After dropping dirt on the coffin, each person returned to his or her car. The grave was filled by the time everyone had left.

I remained, standing alone looking at my burial place. I thought that this was the end. What would happen now? Would I wander for eternity? Was there a future for souls like mine? If yes, when? How? Where? I had too many questions and no answers.

The dark of evening began to fall. The cemetery was empty of people. I suddenly saw various lighted forms hovering over a few new and freshly filled graves. We slowly gathered in one place and looked at each other with curiosity.

I spoke first but not with words. It seemed that we communicated through telepathy. "My name is, or was, David. Have you all recently passed away?"

One answered, "My name is Isaac. I died four days ago. I am waiting to be picked up."

I asked, "Picked up? By whom? When?"

Isaac said, "Since I've been here, I've seen some leave once they were here for seven days. I do not know how, but some that had gone already told me that some entities come for us and then we disappear probably to our last destination."

Another came forward and said, "My name is Ben. It is true that some of us leave after the seventh day, but I am in my twenty-second day, and here I am still wandering. So the seven days doesn't work for everyone."

I said, "It might be because of the way that you died or another reason that you will probably find out soon. Do you leave the cemetery and go see your family?"

Ben said, "I don't have anyone, no family, no friends, but I do go to the places I used to. You can come and go as you wish. But when the time comes, you will know and will return here for the last time."

I knew now that I would be here for at least another six days, went by very fast, so I decided to go back home to see my dear ones for the last time.

My Last Days at Home

I returned home after finding out these latest revelations. Many people were still sitting around tables set up with all kinds of snacks and drinks. The rabbi was sitting at the centre and was discussing Bible passages and religious laws. This was meant to boost my departed soul to a higher sphere so that my soul could depart in peace from this world.

Just after arriving home, the rabbi had taken a pair of scissors and made a cut of a few inches in Sarah's blouse as a sign of mourning to be worn for seven days. After Sarah, it was my father's, mother's, and brothers' turns.

My family sat in low stools, and the rest of the people sat in regular chairs. Many people came and gave their condolences, one after another. It was true that people reading all those Bible passages did me good. The meaning of those passages seemed different now, as if they held a hidden message.

My children sat next to their mother, kissing and holding her, trying to ease her pain and sorrow. They did not comprehend the full impact of what had happened yet. When Lilly saw me, she could not help herself and yelled, "Daddy, you came!" She ran towards me but stopped short when she ran through me. "Daddy, you are funny."

All the assembly looked at her, and many broke into cries at seeing this little girl imagining her departed father and playing with him as if he were there. It was hair-raising and more that Sarah could handle. She exploded in a hysteric cry.

Someone ran and gave her water and tried unsuccessfully to calm her down. All the family were shocked and unable to grasp what was happening.

Dan said, "Sarah needs some space to breathe; please go back to your places."

He was concerned about Sarah's health and Lilly's sanity. He was a good psychologist. Though he had previously told Sarah Lilly having hallucinations was nothing very unusual, her behaviour now seemed very strange. It was not a regular child's game.

This had happened so unexpectedly and so suddenly, as if Lilly really had seen me, that everyone looked in the direction that Lilly was looking as if they expected to see me. It didn't seem that she was faking it. Her facial expression was real.

The rabbi was dumbfounded by the scene. He was very concerned about this little girl. She must have some kind of intuition or connection to higher realms, but now was not the moment nor the place to discuss the matter with her family. They had had enough for today. Maybe it would pass in a few days, and if not, he would check into it.

The guests soon left. After all this commotion, my family members, overtired and having had their share of emotions, went to sleep. All the sofas and folding beds were used. The house was full.

Once my daughter was alone in her bed, I came in and kneeled by her side, smelling her baby perfume that I loved so much. She probably felt me there, and she opened her big blue eyes – the colour of heaven or the deep ocean – which she could see through his heart the infinite love for her.

She said, with a sleepy voice and rubbing her little nose, "Hi, Daddy. You came to tuck me in?"

I said, "As I promised. As long as I am here, I will."

"Why was everyone mad with me for seeing you? I didn't want to make Mommy cry."

"No, princess, you did not make her cry. She is just sad that I am going away for a while; that is the reason, baby."

"I love you, Daddy," she said and closed her eyes.

I stayed for a little while, just contemplating her. I then went to Eric's room and sat for a while and looked at him, my little man. He would be the man of the house and watch over his little sister and mother.

I then went to Sarah's room. She was asleep but clearly disturbed, tossing and turning. I remembered when I met her for the first time. I had fallen instantly in love with her. How beautiful she was – her soft golden hair that fell to her shoulders; her almond-shaped emerald-green eyes that I enjoyed kissing so much; her body like a Greek marble statue, well shaped and with proud breasts that always tempted me. All of her was at the optimum. I had been and continued to be crazy in love with my sweet Sarah, my wife. Since I had met her, I'd only had eyes for her and had never been tempted by anyone else.

She mumbled in her sleep, "David, no … David, please, don't leave; don't leave us … ummm, no, no, noooooooooooooo."

She was having a nightmare, but it was not as bad as the reality. Reality was a nightmare that she couldn't wake up from. I would have given my life for her or my children at any moment. There was nothing I could do to ease her pain. I could not caress or kiss her for eternity.

Why had the Almighty picked me for this terrible and inhuman punishment? I was thirty-five years old, well built with brown hair and blue eyes. Eric was my copy; he looked like a mini-me. Everyone used to say how much we looked alike. I was an architect and loved modern, futuristic designs. They had become my specialty. I had enjoyed my profession and had made plans for a new home that I wanted to build for the family. Even that was gone with this tragedy.

The Seventh Day

The six days had gone by really fast. I was now standing in front of my tomb; the marble stones had already been placed on the ground above my body that lay six feet down. All my family, relatives, friends, and community members were present for the last goodbye.

After the prayers were finished, people began to slowly leave, heads down. Tears dropped from the eyes of all my family members. My father and mother were like zombies, following the rest as if they didn't have a personal say or willpower.

I watched everyone leave with a heavy heart. My Lilly waved shyly at me, afraid to cause another commotion. It did not go unnoticed by her mother, that was worried about her strange behaviour. I waved back and blew her a kiss. This probably would be the last time I would see them. I was stressed about my expected departure tonight towards the unknown.

Night fell rapidly. I remained standing near my tomb, waiting for the imminent. The cemetery was deserted. Here and there, lights appeared above or near certain tombs. There were some new ones, and some others were already gone. Each light stood by his or her resting place, as if waiting for someone or something, some important event, as I did. It was as if we were waiting for a bus for an unknown destination. We stood by our resting places so we could be recognised.

In the Tunnel of Light

The sky suddenly illuminated with lightning, and thunder cracked. It felt as if G-d himself was coming for me, but it was just a thunderstorm. Heavy rain began falling, but I could not feel the wetness or anything.

Towards one o'clock in the morning, a very wide light surrounded me. I was in the middle of it when I perceived three beings of light, what I thought might be angels. For some reason I was calm and not afraid. This was the moment that I had anguished so much about these past seven days. It was also the moment that all humanity had feared since creation, not knowing what comes next. When a person gets to an age to understand, he or she always wonders and asks what happens after we die. There are so many beliefs and disbeliefs about death in our wonderful world.

The beings of light were communicating telepathically with me. We were interconnected by a common wavelength. I now understood that I should not worry and should let myself go. A review of my entire existence passed before me as if I were watching a movie. I saw every important, relevant moment from childhood until my passing from this world, the world of the living. I understood that I was in front of a team evaluating my life, as if I were on trial. There was nothing I could hide from them. I couldn't tell how much time passed; it might have been seconds or hours.

I could not see the cemetery or this world of ours any longer. I slowly arrived at a very long tunnel of light. I understood from the three beings of light that I should go as far as I could, until I could no longer resist the bright light emanating from the end of the tunnel. As I advanced, the light became brighter, and I could no longer see the three beings of light.

The beings of light made me understand that gradually I would know what to do and explained that I would remember my past stay in the world of truth. I then heard or understood, "There are gates on your right and on your left. Do not enter the gates on the left. You will enter to your right only and only when you cannot withstand the brightness of the light. You will then enter to the gate on your right."

I began my journey into the world of light, the dimension where souls waited for their next assignments or reincarnations. That may be too simple of an explanation, but for the moment, that was the only understanding I had.

As I went forward, I noticed the gates on my right and left. Small sparks separated from my being and entered the second and third gates to my right. I knew that they were incarnations that had joined my being since I had been conceived in the material world. Incarnations from other entities often take rides with a main soul in a human to correct the weaknesses of their own souls. These other entities, which some call karma, are sometimes strong enough impulses to influence the main soul to make wrong decisions or behave immorally during his or her existence on earth. The main entity has the moral responsibility to overcome the others' negative influences.

Slowly, as these sparks left my essence, I understood more and more of my situation in this reality. These additives that had separated from me could not continue their voyage because they could not withstand the brightness.

I was now close to the fifth gate. The light was becoming unbearable, but I had to continue as much as I could. My passage on earth was now a remote souvenir. From time to time sparks of light, some small and some bigger, exited through the left gates of the tunnel. I later would find out that these were souls returning for new reincarnations on earth.

As I neared the sixth gate, it became impossible for me to continue my trek. I felt as if I were in an air cushion. I could make no forward movements. I felt no hunger or thirst or any discomfort.

33

In My New World

I finally made the only move I could: I entered the sixth gate. To my stupefaction it felt as if I were coming back home. The gate led not to another tunnel but to the first dimension, a world of its own. It was a world with no material components, no physical bodies. All the people were lights. I could perceive green pastures and trees but, again, not material ones but energies. All the beings, from myself to the plants, were energies of certain purity. There were no homes or cars or anything. It was like the Eden or paradise described in the Bible, but I wasn't quite there yet, as I would find out down the road.

I could recognise family members or, I should say, other souls from the same nucleus. We are all interconnected, and most reincarnations stay within a same nucleus, forming an agglomeration of energies or souls. Now I had my full faculties that I had before going to my last reincarnation. My nucleus, or family, and I were from the same consistency, with the same purity of energy. Just as you cannot connect 100 volts to 200 volts, you cannot mix soul energies. It will cause sparks that will reject each other.

So I was now with my family in the sixth gate or subdivision of the first dimension of four-dimensional existence. Every step or action that we take in the material world reflects in the four dimensions. There are ten sephiroth, or gates. I was in the sixth sephira of the first dimension, but I might be in the third sephira of the second dimension or the second sephira of the third dimension or the first sephira of the fourth dimension. At the tenth sephira of the fourth dimension is the Creator and everything that is part of his light. Nothing can be without his essence, his pure energy intelligence. His essence is called the endless light, which surrounds the entire universe.

The tunnel begins very narrow from the material world and becomes wider the more we advance in it. The light of the Creator becomes brighter and brighter. The mind cannot perceive so much light or energy. This light could blow our minds. We receive it gradually if we try hard enough. This energy would be comparable to taking a human that had lived ten years in total darkness in a cave out to watch the sun at noon. The sun would burn his eyes and blind him forever. This is why souls returning through the tunnel cannot withstand the brightness of the Creator's light past a certain gate. The tunnel directs each soul to its degree of purity. A soul or energy has to be 100 per cent pure to be able to incorporate into the endless light of the Creator in the tenth sephira of the fourth dimension; that is the real Eden or paradise.

The goal is to reach the Creator and not have to return to the material world, where, as G-d told Adam and Eve, "You will derive food from it with anguish all the days of your life. It will bring forth thorns and thistles for you ....By the sweat of your brow you will eat bread."(Genesis 3:17 to 3:23).
The only way to reach the Creator is to return as many times as needed to this material world to cleanse your karma in the material world and not in the world of truth. Only then can you attain such degree of purity.

I was content to be back in my world. Here there was neither time nor distance and no anguish, anger, sadness, or greed. All these were human emotions and were effects of a restricted confinement in a material body. When a soul arrives to earth to reincarnate, it has to be formed of flesh and blood, which are composed of air, water, fire, and earth. These elements are in all living beings, which are subdivided into four categories: humans, animals, plants, and the inert (minerals). In a way a soul cannot operate on earth and is extraterrestrial.

I was now within my nucleus. There were neither days nor nights, but time was probably passing by – days, months, years, I could not tell. Music played all the time. I did not know where it came from, but it was a divine melody. Sometimes we could also hear a faraway murmur, a cry, someone calling for a dear one. I did not know what the cries meant. The only answer I got was that when the time came for me, I would understand and remember. The murmurs could be understood only by the souls that were connected to whatever souls were crying from earth.

We did not speak or ask questions. Knowledge just came to us; some of the information was not available to all in the same degree. Every sephira in each dimension was again subdivided into ten more subdivisions and so on endlessly. Every higher degree had more knowledge than the other and so on. We were on a need-to-know basis.

No one had worries or needs. We just lived in total peace. When your time came to return to your next assignment on earth, you didn't have time to find out; you were just there in a new life form or as an addition to an already existing being. The souls stored in the first sephira of the first dimension can be reincarnated in non-human forms – as animals, plants, and so on. There is so much information to discover that it could take forever to grasp the whole concept and complexity of the universe.

There is in every dimension a master light being, an archangel, that is responsible for the dimension. They are the ones controlling that dimension and are directly connected to the Creator. They decide when and where everyone goes. Under these archangels are master angels or gate masters, light beings that control the individual sephiroth within a dimension, and then there are other light beings below them to control the smaller subdivisions, and so on. This is a simple way to explain the unexplainable in mortal terms.

We are all connected to the universal net of awareness and intelligence. Some are in the lower spheres and some in the higher spheres, but the knowledge is at the grasp of every human being equally. The amount of knowledge gained depends on how much one really desires to obtain the knowledge. A great recipe to progress to the higher spheres is to eliminate the four negative traits that we all carry in our lifetimes: anger, sadness, greed, and pride. Kabbalah study requires the elimination of these four negative behaviours.

Life here was peaceful. We just lived and had no thoughts or worries. We did not have to buy houses or cars. Here, it was just a simple way of living.

We found enjoyment in the music, which was for everyone. The melodies never repeated themselves. The music elevated our souls. Sometimes I could hear what seemed like prayers that included mention of the familiar name David. I couldn't remember what "David" meant, but hearing the prayers did me much good. I was reaching a higher level of knowledge from the universal net. Without thinking about it, I hoped to hear more of these prayers or messages with that name, David.

I was going everywhere with some of my nucleus. This world was beautiful and made my soul rejoice. I was in some kind of ecstasy. It was impossible to reach this feeling with any drug or anything else on the material world called earth.

After a while, even though there were no problems in this world, I felt that something was missing. I couldn't pinpoint what it was until a great event occurred. Heaven opened above us, and we had a wonderful sight of hundreds of thousands of higher light beings praising the Creator, asking him to allow all of us from different subdivisions and dimensions to have a glimpse of his greatness. All of us were in ecstasy. I do not have other terminology to express myself.

Suddenly, heaven lit up with incredible colours as archangels sang melodies. Then seven different grades of angels or beings of light arrived and joined in the song. Each group sang in a different tone. The result was beyond imagination; we were lifted spiritually to heights never reached before.

The culmination of this enlightening moment arrived when we glimpsed the Creator. Millions of pastel colours filled the heavens. No words will ever be able to describe it. The colours slowly became a very bright white light.

We all lowered our ethereal eyes, and each of us was overcome by this unreal happening. Our essence was at maximum heights, and we could not raise our eyes to see again that marvel. After what seemed an eternity, gradually all returned to normal.

I found out that this event was a holiday. And now I also understood what was missing in me. We understood now what paradise was. This demonstration made all of us want to return to the material world to correct our souls (karma), so we would be able to reach the endless light in Eden.

A Short Visit on Earth

Sometime later – I cannot say if it was days, weeks, or months – I heard cries that I understood. A child by the name of Eric called, "Dad, where are you? We need you now. Please, Mummy is not well. She needs you. Please answer me, Dad. Why did you leave us? You had no right to leave us, and also Mummy is waiting for a baby very soon." The boy cried until he fell asleep. His voice seemed familiar, but from where? When?

I knew that if I concentrated I could communicate with that child, so I did. Through his dream I said, "Do not worry, Eric; you will be all right, and your sister and mother will be all right. I will be watching over you. Do not worry; everything will be good."

I did not know who this family was, but I somehow knew the boy had a sister. A gut feeling told me that I had a connection to these children in my past incarnation.

At that moment, I heard a new little voice. "Daddy, this is me, Lilly. You promised me that when I am sad, if I close my eyes and think hard about you, you will come. We are very sad without you, and Mommy is not eating well, and very soon she will have your baby. Please, Daddy, come back. We need you; I need you. You were gone a long time. Please, my daddy, I need to see you."

This little girl's cries made me wonder why I did not recall who they were. I knew for a fact that they were referring to me; if not, I would not have been able to understand them, as I was told or understood. I decided to contact this little girl. Since she was awake, I showed myself as a projection.

When she saw me, her eyes opened wide, and she screamed, "Daddy, my daddy!" Tears came out of her little blue eyes. She ran towards me and through me and fell in the bed just behind me. "You are still funny," she said. "You remember the game we used to play. Daddy, why did you go so long without seeing me?"

Telepathically I said, "I am on a long trip and am too far away to come often. But since you called me, I came." Through my connection with her I knew that I used to call her my princess, so I said, "My little princess, you see, I am doing everything I can. It does not depend on me. I can only do what they tell me to do, but you will be all right. You have a wonderful future, and you will be a great young woman. Your mommy will have a little boy, and she will be fine. All of you will be fine. Your brother Eric will be an architect when he grows up." I was digging the information about her present and future from her through the universal net. I continued, "Now you have to go to bed, and I will tuck you in."

She rejoiced and ran to bed. I came close to her bed and kneeled as I grabbed more data from her memory. "My sweet princess, never despair or feel sad. I will be always here and here." I pointed to her head and heart. I sang a melody that I remembered from heaven. She was all smiles and slowly fell asleep. I felt a pinch where my heart should have been and smiled at this little girl who was already in the world of dreams.

I finally disconnected from this family of mine in the world of the living and returned to my peaceful existence.

***

At seven o'clock the next morning, on earth at the Hirsh's' home, Sarah woke up; she had to prepare the children for school. It became harder for her by the day. She was in her eighth month of pregnancy. She was tired and had been going through life mechanically, not enthusiastically, since David had passed away. A picture of him was next to her side of the bed on the nightstand. She had not been the same since that fatal day when David had been shot. If it were not for the children and the coming baby, she would not have survived.

Now, she stood up, prepared breakfast for the children, and went to wake up Eric first. When he opened his eyes and saw his mom, he said excitedly, "It's weird, but I dreamed of Dad. He told me that everything would be good for us and that we all beok. He looked happy, and he kissed me."

Sarah looked at him; he had many of his father's features. She gave him a poor smile and with a faraway, dim hope in her eyes said, "G-d willing, my darling, it could be a small miracle for our little family. Go take a shower and get ready for school. I am going to wake up your sister." He stood up and went to shower.

Sarah went to Lilly's room. Lilly would be the baby of the house for another month, until the new baby was born. Sarah contemplated her daughter with love; Lilly was so special in many ways. Sarah bent over and kissed her neck as her father used to do. Lilly mumbled with her eyes still closed, "Is that you, Daddy? Are you still here?"

Sarah got choked up. She couldn't make a sound. Her eyes filled with tears. It had been so long since Lilly had spoken this way, and now she suddenly had done it again.

Lilly opened wide her sleepy eyes and saw her mother. "It's you, Mommy. I thought it was Daddy. He came last night to see me. He still loves me and played with me like the last time before he left. He said not to worry and that all of us will be OK. He also said that we will have a little brother."

Sarah said almost crying, "It was a nice dream, baby. I am sure that we will do OK."

"No, Mommy, he was really here. I saw him." She proceeded to tell her mother everything that had transpired the previous night.

"Yes, baby, dreams look real sometimes, like they really happened," Sarah said. She was crying now, and her heart was beating hard. How strange it was that both children had had dreams about their father that same night. Deep down in her heart, she wished that all their dreams came true.

41

In the Meantime

I was back to normal, but I couldn't help but think about the little girl and boy. Why did I not recall anything about my last passage on earth? This was my first time having other thoughts in this world. This family seemed to have suffered from the loss of their father. I must have been him. If not, why had the little girl and boy communicated with me?

All of us in my nucleus could grab here and there some remote information about this family. We were all connected in one way or another to the same families. Some were grandparents or great-grandparents, but we were all loved ones that had departed from the material world. Everyone still had some kind of soul correction to make. No one knew when or where they would reincarnate or whom they would reincarnate as.

The tree of life is very complex. We are all interconnected from the one soul, from the beginning of time, as that tree has developed many branches, and from each branch fruit and leaves have emerged. Some people are as the fruit, and various additional components come from the latter, including seeds, peels, juice, and pulp. Seeds are very important because from them come more fruit trees. But some seeds will make fruitless trees and so on. That is why we are compared to trees and why it's uncertain where our souls will go and in wich entity we will reincarnate.

Of course no one knows, and depending on a soul's previous passage on earth it will get a good or a bad host on its next reincarnation. It is likened to an actor who gets a good role. If he is successful in his first movie, he will get a better one next. Some have leading roles, some have supporting roles, and some have just small parts. Only the ones who work hard will go up the ladder to the top. From the point of view of souls, you move upward from good to great or downward from bad to worse based on your performance. If you did a good job in your previous life on earth, you will get a better life on your next passage through the material world. If you did a bad job, you will come back with less and have a harder life. So the material world is your only asset to show you if you are improving or not.

The material world is an antechamber that leads you up to heaven or down to the other end of the spectrum, hell. Even hell is hard to get into. The people who get into hell are really bad and will no longer get the chance to go back to the material world and upgrade their souls.

Everyone should meditate on all the above and live accordingly. That is what we call free will. When a soul reincarnates on earth, it forgets about its stay in the world of the truth. It leaves by the left gate of the light tunnel, or right on the way down. The second the soul enters a material body, which is composed of the four earthly elements, it comes under the influence of the planets, mostly the Mazzaroth, or the twelve signs of the zodiac. The planets' gravitational powers and effects influence the liquids in the human body, which is about 65 per cent liquid, just as the moon affects tides. The zodiac is divided based on the twelve months of the year, with different influences for each zodiac sign. Because the soul is restricted and in a limited confinement of the body, it is influenced by these zodiac signs.

The soul is no longer directly connected to the celestial world after entering a material body, but the mind can still connect to the universal net and can acquire, in certain cases, higher spheres, interesting and needed information. How can a soul do so? Simply by eliminating the negative emotions of anger, sadness, greed, and pride.

A Special Newborn

It was the ninth month of Sarah's pregnancy. She'd been through hard times since David's death. Her parents and David's parents came to the house to be present for the baby's birth. They all hoped that this little angel would bring some joy to this house, which had been under mourning for such a long time. David's mother and her mother were taking care of the children and the house care because Sarah was too tired and so sad all the time.

Her mother said, "Listen to me, Sarah; you have to give the baby in you womb a chance. It's yours and David's. It is not the baby's fault, what has transpired these past months since David's death. If you continue this way, it puts the baby and you in danger."

"But, Mom—" Sarah started.

David's mother interrupted, "She is right. Your children need you. The baby will need you. Having this baby is like getting David back in a way. This baby is the fruit of your and David's love. So you have to eat and take care of yourself and the baby."

Sarah's eyes were red and tearing. "I am so lost without him. We were as one. But you both are right, and I will listen to you." She hugged and kissed both of them. All three cried, but this time the tears were not only of sorrow but also of happiness.

The children came from school. They were impatient to see what their mommy would have, a boy or a girl. According to Lilly, it was sure to be a boy, because her daddy had told her so. The baby would come any day now, so they had at most a few days to wait to find out. The whole family was excited.

Sarah asked her mother, "Can you come with me to the gynaecologist? I have an appointment at five o'clock."

Her mother said, "Yes, of course," and David's mother offered to take care of the children.

An hour later Sarah and her mother went to the gynaecologist. They had to wait for twenty minutes.

"Good evening, Mrs Hirsh, please come in," the doctor said. He invited Sarah and her mother to sit, which they did, and then he said, "So we are close, any day now. How are you feeling?"

Sarah said, "Quite tired, and I've been having belly troubles lately. My belly has been a lot heavier these past two weeks."

The doctor said, "That's normal; you are in your last week. But let's check you. Please go with Anna."

Anna, the nurse, led Sarah behind the curtain and helped her undress and put on a white blouse. Sarah lay on the consultation bed. The doctor came behind the curtain and listened for the baby's heartbeat with his stethoscope. He tried various times, but worry was painted all over his face.

Sarah noticed that the doctor was checking her too many times. Worried, she asked, "Is something wrong, Doctor?"

The doctor stopped for a moment, and, without answering, he switched on the echograph equipment, spread gel on Sarah's belly, and used the detector. The baby appeared on the screen but was not moving. The doctor tried to detect the baby's heartbeat, but nothing.

The doctor said, "We have to go to the hospital now. I can't hear the baby's heartbeat. We have to performed a caesarean birth"

Sarah's mother, hearing the commotion, went behind the curtain and worriedly asked, "What is wrong?"

The doctor said, "I am sorry. We have to go right now to the hospital. I am very worried. The baby has stopped breathing, and I do not know since when. This is no good, no good!" He kept shaking his head in the negative. "No, no! Anna, call an ambulance!"

Sarah became hysterical and inconsolable, crying very hard. Her mother tried to calm her down but also was crying silently and seemed totally desperate.

Sarah said, "Not again, no, I will not be able to live this again. I will die."

The ambulance arrived and carried Sarah to the hospital. Sarah's mother called the house, and David's mother picked it up. Sarah's mother explained the situation, and David's parents and Sarah's father hurried to join Sarah and her mother at the hospital, bringing the children with them. This would be too much tragedy for this family, in less than a year.

Once at the hospital, Sarah was taken directly to the surgery room. The doctor had called and asked them to make all the preparations. The nurse did not let Sarah's mother in, making her sit in the waiting room. At that moment the rest of the family arrived, and Sarah's mother told them everything that had transpired.

David's mother said, "Oh no, not again! What have we done wrong to G-d? He took our son first and now our grandson?"

David's father said, "We are not sure yet. Let's wait for the surgery to end, and we will then know."

Dan, Sarah's father, said, "Jacob is right. Let's wait and pray for a miracle."

The children were confused. Lilly said, "It's not possible. My daddy told me that we are going to have a baby brother and that we all are going to be OK!"

Sarah's mother hugged both children against her and caressed their heads. All prayed in silence.

In the surgery room, the doctor took the baby out. Sarah was under anaesthesia and unconscious. The doctor held the baby, covered with blood and other liquids, in his hands. The child was inanimate. The doctor said, "He is dead. I do not know what to tell the family. They waited so long for this baby. The mother has been hanging to life by a thread, because of this baby." I don't know if she can take this"?

He laid the baby's body on a small baby bed next to the surgery table and covered it with a white cloth. Sarah was waking up from her sedation. She saw the small body covered with the cloth and did not have to ask. She cried in silence. She'd had a bad feeling even before the visit to the gynaecologist.

The doctor said, "I am so sorry; I really am. There is nothing you could have done differently. Even if you had come when you first started feeling bad, we wouldn't have had different results. Should I call your family?"

Sarah nodded. The doctor went to the waiting room. When all the members of the family saw him and his facial expression, they understood and cried. The miracle had not happened as they'd hopped.

The doctor said, "Sarah needs you all. She is feeling really bad. By the way, it was a boy. Please go and see her, and give her lots of love. Her life depends on it. Please follow me."

They followed as if they were going to jail, their heads down and tears in their eyes. Lilly did not understand the seriousness of the situation. Once inside, they approached Sarah one at a time. They all noticed the little body covered with the cloth.

Lilly asked, "Where is my little brother, Mommy?"

Sarah's mother said, "My darling, he went with your daddy, so your daddy won't be alone."

Lilly said, "This is not true. Daddy promised me that everything would be all right."

When she finally understood that her little brother was gone, she became hysteric. She suddenly entered a rage and screamed, "Dad, you lied to me! Why? I trusted you. I don't love you anymore." She ran to hide in her grandfather's arms and cried her heart out. Everyone tried to calm her down; even Eric came and hugged his sister.

In the Meantime in Heaven

I was, as always, meditating and connecting as much as I could to the universal net. I was trying to understand this family in the material world that had filled my mind.

Suddenly, I heard the cries of the little girl on earth. I heard her scream and call me, or her father, a liar. All my essence became distorted, as if watching a TV without an antenna. I was next to the entrance gate that I had arrived through. Whether it took forever or a second, I don't know, but I was catapulted through the gate and down the tunnel at the speed of a shooting star. On my way down, I crossed many incoming souls. I didn't know what was happening to me or where I was going.

Then I felt myself inside a confined place, and everything around me became suddenly hard as if I were in a tube. I felt the need to breathe and see. It was dark.

***

Lilly said, "Look, there is a big light around the baby."

Everyone else looked but saw nothing. All the electronic equipment went crazy. Suddenly there was a loud baby cry from under the cloth. The nurse removed the cloth. The baby was really crying.

The other nurse ran out and called, "Doctor, Doctor, the baby is alive! Come, hurry!"

The doctor said, "That's impossible. He has not been breathing for hours. No one could survive that."

The doctor returned and asked everyone to leave the room. The family left, except for Lilly, who paid no attention to the doctor's request. The doctor couldn't believe his eyes. Here the baby was, crying and moving his little arms and legs, red from the blood which they had not cleaned after taking him out of the womb.

The doctor said, "This is incredible. This is a real miracle. How can this be? Sarah, this is your miracle. You see, G-d loves you."

Lilly said laughing, "Mommy, I told you. Daddy told me and promised me. You see, he kept his promises."

Sarah took Lilly in her arms and kissed her all over. Everyone else was allowed to come back. Now the room was filled with happiness as they thanked the Lord for this miracle and kissed and congratulated each other. It was as it is in the Jewish prayers: "from mourning to festivities."

The whole hospital found out about the miracle. In the meantime someone was wondering, *What am I doing here? Who are all these people, and what are they celebrating? Who is this lady in white carrying me and cleaning me?* The baby tried to talk but couldn't. Only a cry came out.

The nurse said, "Now that you are clean, come to your mother. She wants to meet you." To Sarah the nurse said, "He weighs 8 pounds and 6 ounces and measures 22 inches." She gave the baby to his smiling mother.

The baby looked at the mother and thought, *Oh my G-d, it's Sarah, my love.* For some weird reason David now remembered his past life as David. "It's me, David," he tried to say, but of course it only came out in baby language. Seeing that no words came out of his mouth, the baby caressed her face.

Sarah said, "Look, look, he is caressing me. Oh, he has David's eyes. He is so cute."

Lilly said, "I love him, my baby brother." She approached the baby.

David looked at Lilly and said telepathically, "My little princess, it's me, Daddy; look at me." He remembered everything from heaven and earth. He was ecstatic that he was alive and with his loved ones. He thought, *Oh my G-d, I am my own son. I remember everyone. I see my dear parents and Sarah's, and here is Eric. I missed them so much.*

Lilly said, "I think he just said to me that he is Daddy!"

All eyes turned towards her and looked at her with a bit of suspicion.

David's mother said, "Your mother said that he has your father's eyes, but he is your baby brother."

Lilly preferred not to continue on the subject until she was alone with the baby. Now she was almost five years old, and Eric eight.

Sarah said, "I think I'll call him Simon. What do you all think?"

They all approved of her choice.

Outside it was like a fair of curiosity. Doctors, nurses, and visitors all came to see the miraculous child. After a short while, even the TV stations came to see the phenomenon baby. The next few days were crazy. Even doctors from other hospitals and professors came to see the miracle child.

Mother and baby finally went home three days later. "Finally, home and some piece of mind," Sarah said.

Her mother said, "Go rest; I will take care of the baby." She tried to take the baby, but he cried. He wanted to be with Sarah only.

"Look, Mom, he always touches my face and my mouth. He doesn't want me to leave him. What if Lilly was right and he is David?" Sarah said with a smile.

51

Her mother said, "I haven't seen you smiling or laughing since that fatal day. You even look more beautiful, darling."

A few days later the ceremonial circumcision was celebrated, and the baby was named – Simon. In the coming days, there were a few happy days and a few calm ones. The new boy brought a breath of fresh air to the family.

About a month later, there was a lot of commotion at the neighbours' house to the right of the Hirshes' house. A lot of family members had arrived and seemed quite happy. Sarah greeted the daughter outside and asked, "How are you? Is someone getting married in your family?"

The neighbour replied, "No, it is my sister, Jane. She had a very bad cancer and had no hope of surviving more than three to four months. But about a month ago, she started getting better. Two days ago, her doctor and various other professionals announced that she is completely cured and that all the damage is gone. They do not understand how this happened. It is for sure a miracle."

"That is great news, fantastic! Please convey my regards to your parents."

The neighbour said thanks and went back to her home. A few days later, another neighbour, the one to the left, experienced a great miracle. The neighbour's five-year-old son had Down's syndrome, but like Jane and her cancer, the disorder slowly disappeared, and the child changed to a normal-looking five-year-old child. That had never happened in the history of that disorder. It was a grandiose miracle.

Simon's miracle and these two seemed too incredible to be true. The three were all treated at the same hospital, Mount Sinai. The media discovered this news, and soon a big crowd gathered on the street where the three families lived side by side. People of all kinds of religious beliefs came. The miracles had revived hope in people that had lost it. The people who gathered were trying to grab a piece of a miracle, a dream. Some prayed. All faiths were present. Some carried pictures of their loved ones that were at the edge of passing from this life. Many wanted to see and talk to the families who had experienced the miracles and ask questions that had no logical answers.

The next day, the house behind the Hirshes' also experienced a miracle. That was too much, and the whole neighbourhood was blocked with cars and caravans trying to get a glimpse of the miracle. Now the situation became unbearable, No one in the neighbourhood could get their cars from their garages or porches.

Since Sarah had been the first to experience a miracle, she came out and gave a detailed story to the press of what had transpired.

The TV anchor asked, "Do you have any advice for the people that are watching?"

Sarah said, "I do not have an explanation. The only thing I can suggest is to not despair and to pray. At least, that was what my family and I did."

The TV crew then interviewed the others who had experienced miracles. Some other neighbours called the police because no one had been able to leave their houses for two days now. The police asked everyone to leave. A few hours later, all the vehicles had left, but a few people still came by feet. The TV stations spoke about the miracles for the next few days.

Two weeks after all the news coverage, after midnight, the ground suddenly started shaking, and a lot of noise came from outside the house. Loud knocks sounded on the front door. Sarah jumped out of bed, her heart beating rapidly. "What is it? What?" She went out to the hallway and ran into her parents, who were still at the house. The noise had woken even Lilly and Eric, whom Sarah told to stay in their rooms. Simon was the only one to remain sleeping.

Dan said, "I will go and see who it is."

Sarah and her parents went down to the ground floor. Dan asked through the door, "Who is it? What is it?"

From the other side someone replied, "This is the FBI and the United States Army. Please open the door at once."

Dan opened the door and asked, "Can I see your badges?"

The two men showed their badges. One was an FBI agent, and the other was a colonel in the Army.

Everyone was in pyjamas, and Dan asked, "What is this about?"

The FBI agent said, "All of you have to come with us."

Dan said, "You did not answer my question."

"We will answer all of your questions at our headquarters," the agent replied.

Sarah said, "But the baby is asleep."

The agent said, "Please go and get him with a blanket but nothing else. We will give you what you need at our headquarters. Let's go now; let's hurry."

"But why?" Sarah asked. "What is going on?"

"Madam, we must leave now. Pick up your child, and let's go," the agent said.

Sarah went and got Simon, Lilly, and Eric and returned to the front door, where her parents were waiting. An officer led them to a black van that was just outside. There were many FBI agents and military personnel that were wearing a special combination suit for protection against chemicals or radiation. They had some kind of equipment and went in the house after the family exited.

The family departed towards an unknown destination. They had thousands of questions and no answers. "What do we have to do with this?" Sarah asked her father.

Dan said, "I have no idea, but do not worry. I am sure that there is a perfectly logical explanation."

Twenty-five minutes later, they arrived at a black glass building in the outskirts of the city and entered the underground parking lot. Once inside, they were taken to a conference room and sat there. Two guards watched over them, but no one had given them a reason for all this.

Two hours later, the FBI officer who had first knocked on their door finally came back. After sitting down, he said, "I am sorry to have made you wait. The reason we have you here is because for the last three weeks our satellites have been disturbed by a strong source of energy coming from your house. We looked inside your home and could not find anything. It will be easier if one of you will tell us where you are hiding that engine or source of energy. Then you can go back home."

Sarah said, "What are you talking about? We have nothing to hide, and we do not know anything about energy or a machine. You said that you searched our home and found nothing. There must be some other explanation, because it's not us. You took us by surprise in the middle of the night; we did not have any time to hide anything."

The FBI officer listened and then, without saying anything, left the room. He said to a man wearing a white shirt, "I don't understand what is going on. This is a normal family, and I don't think that they are hiding anything. I checked the information on all of them. The husband was killed almost a year ago; the wife was pregnant at that time. Her father is a psychologist and has worked all his life as such, and her mother used to be a teacher and is retired now. The rest are children. The problem might be in the satellites."

The man in white blouse said, "To be 100 per cent sure, let's take X-rays of the three adults so we can discard these people as suspe"

The FBI officer re-entered the room and asked Dan, "To be on the safe side, would you, your wife, and daughter consent to having X-rays taken to be sure that you are OK?"

Dan looked at his wife and at Sarah, and both nodded that they agreed. They were taken to the third floor, and one by one had X-rays taken. Everything came out good; there was nothing out of the ordinary.

Once back in the conference room, the FBI officer told Dan, "We are really sorry for what has happened tonight. We will take you back home at once, and we are truly sorry."

The family was taken back home, and everyone went back to sleep. Simon had slept the entire time.

The months that followed were anything but boring. Everyone had the impression that there were some kind of complicity between Lilly and Simon. It was weird to see Lilly speaking to the baby and him looking at her without budging, as if he understood.

A week after the middle-of-the-night FBI visit, Sarah took Simon to the paediatrician for a check-up. He was now two months old. At the doctor's office, a few other people were in the waiting room with their children. For an unknown reason the children quieted down and looked at Simon, and all smiled as if there was some kind of understanding between them. One child that was about five years old said to his mother, "Mommy, my throat and ears don't hurt any longer."

The mother said, "Very good, but we have to see the doctor anyway." She smiled and looked at the other mothers as if he was trying to avoid seeing the doctor.

But to the mother's surprise, another child of about the same age said, "Mother, I have no fever, and my belly doesn't hurt anymore." The mother touched her son's forehead and noticed that he really had no fever, though he'd had a high fever before they'd come. That was unusual.

Then another child told her mother she felt better, and it became hectic. All started talking about how something strange was happening. The nurse came to see what was going on, and the mothers explained what had just transpired.

The nurse said, "I am sure that there is a reasonable explanation for all this," but the mothers did not take this as an answer. The nurse went and informed the doctor.

The doctor came out and said, "Please, ladies, I wish that what you are saying were possible. I will check each child, one at a time, and I will tell you why each child is feeling better if it makes any sense. Please be patient."

Sarah had not said a word as she listened to the mothers discussing this strange situation. For Sarah this was a familiar situation – the strangeness of Simon's birth, then the neighbours' miracles, then the visit from the FBI and the Army, and so on. She had a gut feeling that Simon was at the centre of all the happenings. She wondered if Simon was a very special child with a certain power of healing, but she kept it to herself. One by one the mothers and their children entered the doctor's office. No one left after seeing the doctor, as everyone wanted to see if there were any explanations for these sudden cures.

That was not all. One of the mothers had arthritis, and when she stood up to go in, she exclaimed, "Oh my G-d, I have no pain in my knees! This is a miracle. I've always had terrible chronic pain in my knees when I stand or walk. Something is happening in this office that is curing all of us, even before we see the doctor. How is it possible? Or are we in some kind of frenzy?"

She went into the doctor's office and came back out after a few minutes, followed by the doctor. The doctor cleared his throat and said, "In all my years of medicine, I have never seen such a thing. I really have no explanation for this incredible healing."

Suddenly he saw Sarah and looked shocked. He said to her, "Can you come in please, Mrs Hirsh?"

She stood up with Simon and followed the doctor.

Once in his office he said, "You know, Sarah – can I call you Sarah?"

"Of course, Doctor."

"Since your son was born, Sarah, a lot of unexplained events – let's call them miracles – have been happening. Is this a coincidence? As a man of medicine, I say yes. As a man that has seen many of these 'coincidences' first-hand, I say no, for sure no. It is impossible to find a logical explanation for all this."

"What are you trying to say, Doctor? That my son has something to do with it?"

"I am not saying that at all. I am not in a position to pinpoint how, whom, or what is causing this, but I am sure of one thing at least. I have seen great miracles, and the first one was when your son was born. All the following miracles have happened around you, and that is what directs me to believe that your son is directly or indirectly the centre of all these incredible happenings."

"This is crazy. Are you insinuating that my son is some kind of prophet or that G-d has sent him to cure the sick?" she said in an almost mocking tone. But in her mind, she knew that her son had something to do with what was happening.

The doctor said, "It sounds crazy to me too, but from analysing the results of all that is happening, I think that it is very close."

Sarah said, "Doctor, as you know, I respect and trust you quite a bit as a man of medicine, but you have to keep those thoughts to yourself, at least what concerns my son. I understand that my son's medical secrets must be kept under doctor-patient confidentiality. If you want to discuss your theories with anyone, please do, but please don't even suggest my son. I have suffered enough, and now I am just enjoying my son and my other children."

"I am fully aware of my responsibility as your son's doctor to maintain medical confidentiality. What I am trying to say is that if you allowed me to run some tests on your son and—"

Sarah interrupted, "I am sorry to sound impolite and cut you off, but I do not want to continue on the subject. I do not want to turn my son into some kind of weird fair attraction or religious symbol of any type."

The doctor said, "I do understand, but imagine if your son really has a healing power. He could help a lot of unfortunate, sick children, children who are born with almost nil chances to live more than days or months. Can you understand that?"

"But why my son? He is only two months old. We should let him grow up first, and if he really has such powers, we will think about it then. Anyway, I will explain this to my family. I'm not promising anything, but I will let you know."

The doctor stood up, followed by Sarah. He thanked her, and she left. Sarah thought about what the doctor had said. He was right in one way: if Simon was really gifted, he could help many unfortunate children. But then he would have a very hard life. She would discuss it with her parents and in-laws, who were in town for a visit, once she arrived home.

The doctor was thinking about this special child and his gift of life to others. This would be the first case like this ever. He hoped that Sarah would change her mind and would do the right thing.

Of course, it was all supposition, and he was not sure of anything. The tests could confirm his theory.

Later, at home, Sarah sat down in the living room. She seemed distracted by her thoughts, and her mother asked, "What is wrong? You look worried. What did the doctor say?"

Sarah's parents and David's parents gathered around her in the living room around the coffee table.

Sarah explained what had transpired at the doctor's office and all her worries.

David's father said, "This maybe explains Simon's birth and what has happened to all the people that have come close to him. Even I feel a lot better since his birth."

Sarah's mother said, "But the child's life will be very difficult and unbearable, and he is only a small baby."

Sarah said, "That is exactly what I told the doctor. But if this theory is real, we could help many children. So I am confused and undecided."

David's mother said, "Simon was born dead without a soul, and G-d gave us a second chance and gave him one. If the Lord did that, how can we refuse to share this gift?"

Sarah's father said, "To me, it is still hard to believe that Simon has such healing powers. But let's assume that he does. This will affect all his life from childhood to the end and in a way will affect our lives too. But we have to hear what the doctor has in mind. If his plan is just to bring Simon in on certain cases, like the ones where someone's life is in danger, then maybe it would be possible to bring Simon to those places with no one having to know who he is. So neither he nor us, his family, will have any problems. What do you all think?"

Sarah said, "Good thinking, Dad. If it is possible this way, with no one knowing who he is, then I am going to go for it. Of course this is if Simon has such healing powers. I will call the doctor and invite him over."

They all nodded in approbation. Sarah called and asked to speak to the doctor. When the latter heard that it was Sarah, he told his secretary to pass the call to his office and said, "Do not pass any other calls."

The doctor said, "Hi, Mrs Hirsh. What can I do for you?"

"Hello, Doctor," Sarah said. "I'm calling about the subject that we discussed this morning. Could you to come to my home so we can discuss the possibility of accepting your suggestion? My parents, parents-in-law, and I will be present."

"Great! It will be my pleasure. I knew that you would give this matter a second thought. When is good for you? I am free tonight after 7 p.m."

Sarah said, "That will be fine."

"See you this evening, bye." The doctor hung up, feeling a bit optimistic about the possible continuation of his suggestion.

Sarah said to her parents and parents-in-law, "That's it. He will be here after 7 p.m., and we will know then what kind of tests he wants to perform on Simon."

At that moment Eric and Sarah arrived home from school. "Hi, Mom," they said in unison. "We are hungry." They came and kissed Sarah and their grandparents.

Lilly said, "I want to see D … the baby. Where is he?"

Sarah said, "He is asleep; do not wake him up."

"OK, Mommy, I will see him later."

Eric and Lilly went to eat in the kitchen with David's mother while Sarah's parents and David's father discussed how to protect Simon and what conditions they should request from the doctor.

It was 7 p.m. exactly when the doorbell rang. Eric was the first to open the door. David's father was just behind him.

David's father said, "Hello, Doctor, I am David's father."

The doctor said, "How are you sir?"

Sarah said, "Hi, Doctor. Welcome to our home; come in please."

They all followed Sarah to the living room. To the children she said, "Please go to your rooms. Do your homework, and do not make noise that will wake Simon."

Once the children had left, Sarah's parents and David's mother shook hands and made acquaintance with the doctor. Then the adults all took seats around the table, and the doctor said to Sarah, "Well, I was half surprised by your call. I knew that you couldn't shut your eyes to other people's suffering. Please, do tell me what you have in mind."

Sarah said, "Well, we all discussed and gave serious thought to your idea of helping other children with Simon. We have some questions. First, what kind of tests do you have to do to Simon? Second, how do you intend to use his healing power, if he has any? Third, will he be in contact with contagious people? Fourth, how will you hide his identity? Fifth, for how long do you want to use him? Sixth, can all this affect his health in any way? That's about it."

The doctor took note of everything that Sarah asked and replied, "I understand exactly what you are asking and will answer in the order you asked. First, the tests will be simple. I will put him in a room close to the rooms of children that are ill. Based on what I have noticed and what has happened around your house, the ill children should not need close contact to Simon. Already here at the hospital various cases have been cured this way. That answers your second question too. Third, he will be in a single room by himself, so no contact with contagious people. Fourth, I will give him an alias, so no one will know his identity Fifth, I do not know how long we will do this. Time will tell. Sixth, I do not think it will affect his health. I will examine him from time to time, and if anything worrying happens, I will stop immediately. Do these answers satisfy and ease your worries?"

Sarah said, "Just about. I am not 100 per cent calm, but the best way to find out is to start. When would you want to begin?"

The doctor said, "We can start as soon as you decide. For me we could start tomorrow."

Sarah said, "It's OK with me. Dad, Mom, Jacob, Esther, what do you say?"

They all nodded in approval. After they all had drinks, the doctor stood up, shook hands with all present, thanked them for their cooperation, and left.

Simon asked Lilly, telepathically of course, to come to him. Lilly went to Simon's crib in her mother's room. Simon, with his eyes wide open, said, "Lilly, it's me, Dad."

Lilly laughed and said, "You are so small, Daddy, but I know that it is you. How is it that you came back so small? And you are also my baby brother! It's so funny." She giggled.

"Listen, my darling, I cannot explain everything to you now, but I know what your mother and the doctor want to do by taking me to the hospital every day. Your mother has to stop this."

"But, Daddy, I don't know anything about this."

63

"Lilly, please tell her what I just told you. If she goes through with this plan, there could be a big problem. It could be exceedingly bad."

"I will tell her, but I know that she won't believe me," Lilly said.

"Go now and tell them, please, my baby."

Lilly was amazed by how this little thing communicated with her. His tiny lips barely moved, making only tiny sounds of a normal baby, but she heard a different voice directly in her mind. She was only a five-year-old little girl; it was too much for her. But she trusted blindly the voice of her father.

She said, "I will go now, Daddy." She ran out of the room and down the stairs to the living room, where all the family was still discussing the matter.

"Mommy, Mommy," Lilly said, "I was talking to Dad ... I mean Simon, and he told me to tell you not to do what the doctor wants to do."

They all looked at each other, not believing what they'd heard from Lilly's mouth.

Sarah said, "What are you saying, baby? Simon is a baby; he doesn't speak yet. Do not pretend; this is a very serious conversation. How did you hear what we said? You were in your room."

"I swear, Mommy, the baby is Daddy. He called me and told me what I just told you. Why don't you believe me? He said that it will be very bad if you do what the doctor wants." Lilly began crying. She couldn't understand why no one believed her.

David's father said, "Come, my baby, please don't cry. You see, what you mother said is that the baby cannot talk. He is so tiny, but one day he will talk. You were playing with Simon?" He wiped her lovely childish face.

"Grandpa, I swear that everything is true. I'm not lying," she said sobbing.

David's father said, "It's late, my darling. I will take you to bed, and I will tell you a story. Do you want to do that?"

Lilly nodded. He picked her up and carried her to her bed. She was already asleep by the time he got to her room. He laid her in bed, covered her, kissed her forehead, and switched of the main light, leaving a little lamp on.

He went down, where everyone was waiting. They looked at him as he came down the staircase. All were really worried about this. It had been a while since Lilly had spoken weirdly.

Sarah was the first to speak. "Dad, I am really worried about Lilly. She hasn't talked this way in a long time. How did she hear our conversation? She was in her room; I am sure of it."

Sarah's father said, "Do not worry, darling. I will talk to her tomorrow, and I will see, OK? Let's all go to sleep; it is almost midnight."

They all stood up and went to their respective rooms.

The First Day at the Hospital

Sarah couldn't sleep that night. She was too excited and nervous about the test that could change their lives and also about what had transpired with Lilly. Lilly had been right before, but it had been a while since she'd last behaved that way.

This whole matter seemed unreal and far-fetched, though she herself had witnessed a lot of unexplained occurrences. She tried hopelessly to chase all these thoughts from her mind. She got up at 6.30 a.m., took a shower, and went to wake up the children so they would be ready for school.

She first went to Eric's room. She looked at him tenderly. He looked so much like his father. She kissed his forehead and said, "Wake up, my big boy. It's time to get up. Go take a shower."

Eric stretched and said, "It's too early, Mom. Let me sleep another ten minutes, please?"

"Ten minutes will not change a thing, darling; let's go." She pulled off his sheets and helped him up.

Once he was up, she went to Lilly's room. Sarah looked at her mysterious little girl tenderly. She looked so sweet with her little nose, freckles, big eyes, and long lashes. Sarah thought, *What is going through this gorgeous little head? How does this little girl, barely over five years old, come up with these strange statements and ideas? She loved her father beyond comprehension. Maybe that is the reason for this strange behaviour.*

Lilly looked like a little angel. Sarah kissed her tiny nose and each eye and gently hushed in her ear, "Good morning, little girl. It's time to wake up for school." She had to repeat herself three times before Lilly scratched her nose and opened one eye. She looked at her mother, gave a poor smile, and said, "Hi, Mommy. I was dreaming of Daddy. He is unhappy that you are taking him to the doctor. He said not to last night. Are you still mad with me?"

"No, my little angel, how can I be mad at you? You know that I love you very, very, very much. But dreams are only dreams, my love; they are not real."

"But I was awake and not dreaming when Daddy told me that you shouldn't go to the hospital. Why don't you believe me? I never lie."

"OK, baby, it's time to take a shower and go to school. We will discuss it after school, OK?"

Lilly was not happy that no one believed her. She stood and went to the shower with a long face, not looking at her mother.

Thirty minutes later, everyone was in the kitchen having breakfast.

Sarah's mother said, "Sarah, let me go with you."

Sarah said, "OK, Mom. You want to join us, Esther?"

Esther said, "Of course. I have nothing else to do. The men can take the children to school and go to buy groceries and whatever we need."

The men nodded in approval.

The women left for the hospital with Simon. Once there, the doctor welcomed them and said, "Good morning, ladies. I will not hide from you that I was and am very excited about this. Are you ready?"

Sarah said, "Yes, I hope that you will not be disappointed."

He smiled and asked them to follow him. They took the elevator to the top floor to the paediatric section. A room was ready for

Simon. He was checked in as a patient for a general check-up. There were two armchairs, and the doctor went and got an additional chair. A single bed for a child was in the room. The blinds were down to avoid curiosity. One nurse only was in confidence, and she worked solely for the doctor.

The doctor took Simon from Sarah's arms and laid him in the bed. They all noticed that Simon looked weird. If he wasn't a baby, the doctor would swear that he was angry and unhappy. Though Simon had a strange upset adult expression, he did not cry.

The doctor said, "Would you like coffee, drinks, anything?"

Sarah said, "Water will be fine, thank you."

The doctor told the nurse to bring a bottle of water and left.

Hours went by. For the women it was boring. They had long talks but then ran out of subjects. Soon it was one o'clock in the afternoon, and they were hungry. The nurse arrived and brought sandwiches and drinks.

Sarah said, "Thank you, that's very kind. How is it going? We haven't seen the doctor, not even once."

The nurse said, "We have had emergencies all morning. The moment he frees himself, he will come to see you."

"Is everything all right?" Sarah asked.

The nurse said, "He will explain when he comes. Sorry, I have to rush."

She left without any further explanation. That worried Sarah and the mothers.

Sarah said, "I feel something is very wrong, and I am sure that it has to do with Simon."

68

Sarah's mother said, "Don't be so negative and dramatic. I'm sure that it has nothing to do with Simon, and it is only a hospice ..."

At that moment the doctor entered the room. He was pale and looked distressed, not knowing where to start.

"What's wrong?" Sarah asked in a trembling voice, clearly anxious and worried.

The doctor said, "I ... I ... don't understand. It is a catastrophe. All is wrong, very wrong ... I do not know how or where to start."

Sarah said, "What? Please explain."

The doctor said, "After I left you this morning, things looked great. Children began getting better. Some who had been in comas regained consciousness, and others who had been in their last moments suddenly requested food and were smiling for the first time in months. I was so happy and was about to come and tell you when the administration called all the surgeons and medical staff to an urgent meeting in the conference room.

"The head of the hospital told us that we had an epidemic emergency. We have a ward that holds inmates from a state prison. Something happened, and of the thirty-one men and women, seventeen of them died suddenly, despite not having life-threatening conditions. They all died in the space of an hour, without any logical explanation.

"That's not the only problem; we had the same problem in most of our departments. Some patients got better, and some that were not terminally ill died. Even some people that came to visit other patients died.

"The head of the hospital already called the Centers for Disease Control and Prevention in Atlanta. The hospital is in quarantine, and no one can leave or enter. This is a catastrophe. This is a big problem, and we do not even know what we are facing. The

69

hospital head instructed us to take all the people that look all right and separate them in the lobby and hurry."

The phone rang; the doctor answered, listened, said OK, and hung up. "The CDC team has arrived. Let's all do what we have to do and help the team with any of their requests."

Sarah and the ladies listened attentively and did not interrupt the doctor, who looked devastated. He continued, "I am very worried that Simon could be the cause for all this, and I do not understand the deaths. Simon has the power to heal, not to kill, so it must be another reason. Please do not leave the room until the CDC tells us to."

Sarah said, "But my children will be coming back from school. I need to pick them up and feed them."

The doctor asked, "Can you call your father or father-in-law?"

"I suppose so," Sarah said, "but how long do we have to stay here?"

"The moment I hear the quarantine is lifted, I will come to notify you. Please excuse me; I have to go," the doctor said and left the room.

Sarah was stunned. Lilly's words came back to her mind and how she'd insisted that she wasn't lying about her dad telling her this would be very dangerous. She'd even cried. *That is totally crazy. How can this be?* Sarah thought.

Meanwhile, Sarah's mother called Dan. After hanging up she said, "Your father will pick up the kids. He and Jacob were very worried about us, but I calmed them. They heard about the situation here in the hospital on the news. All the TV and radio stations are talking about it."

Sarah switched the TV on, and there it was: the news reporter was on the scene at the hospital. The hospital was surrounded by the

Army and people in white hermetic decontamination suits with masks.

A man in a white shirt was talking to the news reporter and trying to calm the situation. He said, "I am Dr Smith from the CDC of Atlanta. We have done many tests and have not found any contamination or viruses in the hospital. The deceased people seem to have died of natural causes. It sounds unreal, but we have done various autopsies and have found nothing – no poison, no contamination of any kind. Ten highly renowned professors from all over the United States and from this hospital haven't been able to find the reason for so many natural deaths in one single hospital."

The newsman asked, "How many people have died?"

Dr Smith replied, "Forty-five men, thirteen women, and two children, all different ages, nothing in common. We will keep the people inside another twenty-four hours to be sure that all the rest are in good health, and then they will be released."

"This sounds impossible to believe, that sixty people would decide to die all together, in the space of a few hours. Saying the deaths were due to natural causes sounds like a ridiculous excuse. You cannot ask the people to believe this nonsense, with all due respect, Doctor."

"I understand your pessimism," Dr Smith said, "but how can we explain those thirty-nine children and twenty-one adults who were cured of various types of serious illnesses in the same period? For this we also do not have a reasonable explanation."

The news reporter said, "So, summarising, sixty died, and sixty others experienced miraculous cures. This sounds like science fiction."

Someone came and mumbled something in the newsman's ear. His eyes opened widely, and he said, "I was just reminded that this same hospital was the scene of other unexplained 'miracles.' Now we have some new thoughts to investigate."

Sarah nervously switched off the TV. She was shaking and crying. "Now there will be all kinds of investigations, and they will get to us, to Simon, and that is precisely what we wanted to avoid."

The doctor entered the room and said, "I presume that you all watched the news."

Sarah, still crying, nodded. Surrounded by the two mothers, she said, "You see, Doctor, this was what we were worried about before I accepted your offer. Now they will see Simon as a circus phenomenon. To tell you the truth, my daughter, Lilly, was against it. She said that her dad told her that it would be very dangerous to come here. It is just as she said."

The doctor said, "All that has happened after Simon's birth has no reasonable explanation, and it is beyond my expertise or common sense. I can promise you that I will not tell anyone about what we have done today. Please have patience; they will let us go soon enough. I will send food and drinks with the nurse. Just try to relax."

David's mother said, "He is right. Relax, my daughter; you are all shaken up. Believe me, we all are. I have an idea; you should all come to our home in Florida until this matter quiets down."

Sarah, without thinking, said, "I accept. The moment they let us leave the hospital, we will take a few things, and we will go."

Sarah's mother also accepted the invitation. Before the day ended, the CDC had released everyone from the quarantine, and Sarah and her family went home.

Once home, they discussed what had transpired at the hospital and what they had decided to do. They all left for a while to Florida. David's father was delighted to have them all at their very large home in Boca Raton.

Five Years Later

In the beginning Sarah's intention was to stay in Florida for just a short while, but the hospital investigation became too pressing, and too many questions were left unanswered.

Sarah and the family were confused about Simon's healing powers, but what about the deaths? She did not know what to think about them. She had some kind of fear of Simon even though he was her son and she loved him dearly. He was the fruit of her love with David. How could Simon be bad and cause death?

She tried to chase these negative thoughts out of her mind, but they came back in force. Slowly, she developed a fear of her own child. At night she was scared. It was crazy and unthinkable. Simon looked at her not like a child at his mother but with a strange expression.

Since the family was worried about the consequences of the investigations, they gradually decided to stay and live in Boca Raton. David's parents did everything in their power to make them feel comfortable and wanted. The children were registered at school under Sarah's maiden name, and she kept Simon at home. Slowly things returned to normal, and routine took over.

Five years passed, and Simon was now five and a half years old. Sarah did not send him to school for fear that things would get out of hand and they would have to move again. Sarah taught him at home. He was a very quiet child for his age and spoke wisely, like an older person.

Lilly was already nine years and five months old, and Eric twelve and seven months. Lilly and Simon were inseparable.

One day, Simon said, "Sarah, let's all go to the movies. I am tired of being at home."

Sarah said, "I told you to stop calling me Sarah; I am your mother."

"Is Sarah not your name?" Simon asked.

"Yes, but you are a little boy, and to show me respect, you should call me Mother or Mommy."

"If it makes you happy." Simon sometimes had very straight answers, but sometimes he could be a normal cute child.

What no one knew was that Simon had an adult's mind. He knew quite well his peculiar situation, but he kept it to himself. He had two full personalities, one as David with all his memories as Sarah's husband and father of Lilly and Eric and the other as his soul, his celestial entity, that came and went as it pleased. In another way it was in control of Simon's being. There was no space for Simon, the child.

Simon did not confide in anyone but Lilly. She knew that he was her father. It sounded weird, but it was the case. David was in constant pain from not being able to tell his loved ones who he was. The problem was that they would take him to a psychiatrist. He would have loved to scream from the rooftops that it was him, but his celestial entity would not let him. His celestial entity was the one to decide.

Simon asked, "So, Mommy, can we go to the movies? Please?"

Sarah said, "I think that sounds good, my love. Hey, kids, what do you think?"

The kids all agreed. The grandparents preferred to stay home.

They went to the movies. They were happy to go together, but Sarah was afraid of any uncontrolled happenings. They rarely went out with Simon. She usually brought children's movies home, but Simon never liked them and would fall asleep. Then and only then did he look like a tender child.

In the theatre, Simon sat next to Sarah and held her hand. It felt as if they were an odd couple. He would kiss her hand from time to time and look at her tenderly. She looked at him, amazed at her little boy that seemed in love with his mother. He reminded her so much of David. The thought that he could be David, as Lilly had said so many times, was crazy and impossible. She quickly chased the thought out of her mind.

The movie started, but Simon kept looking at Sarah. She felt uncomfortable, but what else could she do? She could feel his tender look, childish and at the same time loving. She was sure about it. She thought, *Oh, David, is it you? Please give me a sign.*

At that moment, Simon took her hand to his lips, smiled at her, and kissed it again. She swore that she recognised David in him. Maybe it was her wishes and love for David that made her feel this way. Spectators and children were laughing at the cartoon movie. The only child not laughing was Simon. He couldn't take his eyes off his mother.

Suddenly, Simon got a faraway look in his eyes. He released Sarah's hand, stood up, and went to a man in the front row who had a little girl sitting on his lap. The girl looked scared and was crying quietly. The man took his hands off the little girl and looked at Simon, who seemed very angry. Simon pulled the little girl, who was probably his age, out of the man's reach.

The man looked at Simon intrigued, without saying a word or trying to hold the child. He couldn't take his eyes off of Simon's eyes. Suddenly the man yelled his lungs out, a scream that gave everyone the chills. A fire broke out over his body, and he began burning alive. In a matter of seconds, the lights of the theatre came on, and people began rushing out. Simon pulled the little girl to join Sarah, who was frozen from the scene. Simon rushed out of the theatre with the little girl, followed by his brother, sister, and mother. All the doors were open, and the fire department arrived in a matter of minutes.

Sarah looked at Simon and asked, "What was all this about? Who is this little girl? What happened over there?"

Simon said severely, "That man is not her father but her stepfather, and he has been hurting her in a very bad manner, if you know what I mean." Simon was not the gentle Simon from ten minutes ago. His face showed not just anger but pure disgust.

A police officer and a fireman came to Sarah and asked, "Are you all OK?"

Sarah said, "Yes, thank you, just a scare. This little girl is not mine. I think that the man with her is the one that caught fire. We pulled her out with us."

The policeman said, "That was very courageous of you. You probably saved her life."

He asked the little girl who she was, but she seemed to be in shock and didn't seem to understand what he was asking.

He then turned to Sarah and asked her, "Can you please come with us so we can take your statement?"

Suddenly Sarah felt trapped; if the police investigated them, they would discover who they were. She said, "Please, my children are in shock, and I would like to take them home. Can we do it tomorrow?"

The police officer said, "I am sorry, but we need to do it now that the memory is still fresh, and we do not know who the little girl is. Please, it will take only a few minutes."

Sarah nodded, took her children, and followed the officer to his car.

Sarah called her father and explained in short what was going on without mentioning Simon's role. Once at the station, the captain invited Sarah into his office, saying the children could sit on a bench just outside his door. Sarah was very nervous about Simon being there when she was unable to control him. Before she entered, she instructed Simon not to move a finger and told Eric and Lilly to watch over him. Her eyes expressed the importance of their task.

The captain said, "Do not worry; an officer will watch over them. So what happened at the movies?"

Sarah said, "Well, we were watching the movie, and everyone was laughing. Then suddenly I saw fire coming out of a man two rows in front of us. As he screamed, I noticed the little girl standing a few feet from him, unable to move, frozen. I ran to get her and told my children to run out, and I followed them. The fire department came in, and that's it. You know the rest."

The captain asked, "Did you know this man or little girl before? Or do you know her name?"

"No, we rarely come to this theatre, and I have never seen him. I'm sorry I can't help you more."

The captain said, "I really appreciate your help." He made a sign to his secretary, who had transcribed everything Sarah had said. The secretary handed the statement to him, and he showed Sarah where to sign and to write her name, address, and phone number. Sarah used her maiden name and gave her parents' address in Chicago, in order to avoid giving her Florida adress and her mobile phone number. He thanked her again. He did not give much importance to her statement, saying it was just a formality.

Outside two policemen were watching a man in handcuffs. He looked very sad and desperate. Simon, who was a few feet away, looked at him and went up to one of the officers. "Officer?" he said.

The officer said, "Yes, kid, what do you need?"

"This man here is not the killer. The killer's name is John Bender, and he is also a police officer."

Eric pulled Simon away, stopping him from saying more. The officers and the suspect looked at Simon, unable to believe their eyes or ears.

At that moment Sarah came out of the office. Seeing Simon close to the officers, she went and picked him up in her arms right away. She said to the officers, "Sorry, my son is a little confused from the accident."

The captain asked another officer to take the family back to their car at the theatre, and they all left.

The captain asked the two officers, "What was that about?"

"You won't believe it, Captain. The kid came to us and said that this guy," one of the officers said, pointing to the arrested man, "is not guilty and did not kill the woman. He said that a guy by the name of John Bender is the killer and that he is also a police officer."

The captain said, "He is just a five-year-old kid; don't pay attention to it."

The officer asked, "So how did he know about the woman's murder and the name of this officer?"

"Maybe he heard you talking about it, and he probably got the name from the movie he just saw. Children have vivid imaginations."

"But, boss, he—"

"I said forget about it. Take him to a cell."

The captain thought, *How does the kid know about this? How does he know Bender?* The captain knew exactly the whole story.

Bender, who worked in another district, and the captain were accomplices, and Bender had indeed committed the murder – under the captain's orders. The woman had been the captain's lover and had heard many of his conversations about thefts and murders that he and Bender had committed for money. The woman had known too much and had been talking too much, even hinting that she wanted a share of the money. So he'd decided to get rid of her.

The captain called Bender. "We have to meet; it's urgent. Tonight, 10 p.m. at our usual place." He hung up.

Once at home Sarah explained to her parents and parents-in-law everything that had transpired since they'd left for the movies. She said that Simon had probably caused the incidents.

Sarah's father asked, "But how did he burn the man?"

No one was paying attention to Simon, so he said, "Can you all listen to me?" His face looked strange, unlike a child's. "I did not do anything to that man, He was doing very bad things to the little girl, and when I am in presence of evil people, they just die. I didn't do anything. He got what he deserved."

Everyone listened, unable to believe what he had said. This was the first time that he'd spoken about his powers. He spoke like an adult; his facial expression was serene but different. In other words, he looked and sounded like a tiny five-year-old man. They all thought that he had a double personality.

Sarah asked, "Simon, what were you talking to the police officers about?"

Simon said, "That man they'd arrested was not guilty of the murder he'd been charged with. A guy named John Bender, who also is a police officer, is the one who killed the woman."

They all looked at each other, horrified at Simon's statement.

79

David's father said, "But, my boy, your mother told you not to talk to people. That will bring us troubles."

Sarah's father said, "I hope that they did not pay attention to a five-year-old child."

Sarah said, "But he gave the name of an officer and revealed that he knew that the man had been arrested for the murder of a woman. If this officer is known, then we will have a bit of a problem. I gave my maiden name and a mobile phone number and your address in Chicago. Let's hope that in the event that this thing arouses interest, we will have time to decide what to do."

Sarah's father said, "Disconnect that mobile phone immediately, and remove the battery. If we don't, they can easily locate us."

Sarah did so immediately, as if the phone was about to explode, and said, "It was too good to be true. We've lived five years in peace. I hope that we are not going to have to move again."

Simon was listening as a grown-up and said, "Mommy, you do not have to worry. I am here, and no one can touch you. The moment they think about doing something bad to us, I will know."

They all looked at him, not believing what he was saying. It came out of his lips, but it sounded as if it came from an adult. Even the voice did not sound remotely like Simon. They were left speechless.

Sarah said, "My love, how do you know all this? You are just five y—"

Simon cut her off. "I know, but I know things and can do things. I cannot say more than that for the moment."

"But are you my son?"

They all probably had been thinking the same question but had not dared to ask or had been afraid to find out.

Simon said, "Of course I am your son, but at the same time I'm more than that. In time you will know everything." Suddenly his facial expression changed radically, and he said, "Mommy, I am hungry."

The only one who knew everything was Lilly, but no one had paid attention to what she'd said in the past.

Sarah's mother said, "Come, my love, I will serve you and you too, Eric and Lilly."

The children followed their grandma to the kitchen. Simon now looked and behaved like a normal five-year-old child.

When Sarah and the parents were alone, David's father seemed more than intrigued and said, "Maybe Lilly was right from the beginning; maybe Simon is David!"

Sarah said, "Now that you mention it, at the movies, Simon held my hand and kissed it at various times and looked at me most of the time. I felt embarrassed. My G-d, could it be possible that David has been reincarnated in our child?"

In the meantime, the captain was on his way to meet Bender. He was now very concerned about this unexpected complication. He and Bender had been eliminating various drug dealers and stealing their merchandise and money. Every time, they had found the perfect guilty person to blame as the criminal. They were real dangerous murderers with badges. He finally arrived at the place they always met, a bar that belonged to them.

Bender had already arrived, and the captain said, "Hi, Bender."

Bender asked, "What was so urgent?"

"We have a problem. I don't know how, but a little kid spoke to one of my officers and gave your full name as being the murderer of Nancy. He also said that the sucker we got is not guilty. What do you say about that?"

"How can this be possible? I was in the Everglades, and I left no trace. It is a shame that the alligators did not eat her completely. The head was left and one hand. But there were no witnesses for miles around. There were no hiding places. I am 100 per cent sure."

The captain said, "Damn, how does he know? And he had no doubts about it." He pulled a sheet out of his pocket and gave it to Bender. "Here is the mother's info; we have to find out more about this."

Bender looked at the sheet and said, "What is this statement for? Who burned the old man?"

"No one killed him. It was an internal combustion according to the coroner. But this old fart was a paedophile and probably molested his stepdaughter. I wish he was alive; we could have used him as another guilty bastard for our business."

"What do we do now? Kill everyone who knows?"

The captain said, "I do not like killing children, but investigate first, and then, if we have no choice, we will find a way to make it look like an accident. Well, I have to go; I'm tired. You do what you have to do. Goodnight."

He stood up and left. Bender stayed a while longer sipping his whisky. He was thinking about this new thing that had just popped up. How was this possible? Was the captain trying to set him up? Lately he had not been able to trust anyone, not even his own mother. He looked at the woman's statement that the captain had given him. The address was in Chicago and not in Florida, and she didn't list car plate numbers. So the only thing left was the phone number.

He pulled an unidentifiable mobile phone out of his pocket and dialled the number. As he'd supposed, no one answered, and there was no voicemail set up.

He called his precinct and said, "Hi, it's me. Check this number, and call me back. It's urgent."

Ten minutes later, his phone rang. He picked up and said, "Yes?"

A guy on the other end said, "The number is for the type of phone that you can buy without providing identification. I tried to locate the phone, but it's impossible because the person has taken out the battery. Sorry."

Bender did not like that at all. He thought, *This stinks. I can smell the set-up.* He began imagining all kind of scenarios. Probably the captain had gotten caught and was cooperating with the FBI. A nervous tic made his eye twitch from time to time. What should his next move be? What should he do?

The idea that a five-year-old boy had been a witness to the murder was ridiculous. What would a kid of that age have been doing at one in the morning – in the Everglades of all places?

He decided to make one more move. He called one of his contact, Jerry, who worked at the FBI head office at Quantico. He knew that getting Jerry's help would cost him, but Jerry would be very discreet.

"Hello," Jerry answered. "Who is it?"

Bender said, "It's me, John. How are you?"

"OK. And you?"

"Can you check this name for me – Mrs Sarah Adler? It's in Chicago. I needed it yesterday." He also gave Jerry the address. "When can I have it?"

"Tomorrow."

"Can you also check if anyone was asking about me or my friend the cap?"

"You got it. Don't forget my gin," Jerry said, meaning money.

Bender said, "OK, Jerry, talk to you tomorrow," and he hung up.

Back at the house, all were asleep but Sarah and her father.

Sarah said, "Dad, I am really worried. What if what Simon said is true? We are in danger."

Her dad said, "Tomorrow is a new day. We can talk more then. Why worry now? Let's go to sleep; it is past midnight."

Sarah stood up and kissed her father, and they went to their respective rooms.

The next morning was not a usual one. Sarah was not in a great mood. She hadn't slept much. She decided to let the children stay home from school for a few days, to let things quiet down.

Sarah said to the grandparents, "Let's go to Key West for a couple of days. We can take your caravan, Jacob. Is it OK with you all?"

Jacob said, "It's OK with us. Dan, what about you?"

Dan said, "Why not? Let's enjoy some time with the children."

Sarah said, "Great! Let's move."

At that moment the children came down from their rooms, and Sarah said, "Children, you are not going to school today. We are going to Key West for two days. We will all be together and can enjoy each other's company. What do you think?"

Lilly said, "Great! It will be fun." She looked at Simon with a mischievous smile. "Simon, we will have fun!"

Strangely Simon was not of the same idea, he had a weird feeling. He was grumpy and very disturbed by this decision. "Mommy, what you are doing is ridiculous and will not help at all. These

two days will be the time they need to find us, and then what?"
What he said and the way he said it, left them totally speechless.
He spoke like a man and not a five-year-old child. He was right,
and what he said made sense. He probably had some kind of clue,
though, the way he and only he could have. Simon continued,
"They will find us, and soon. Let them. We have done nothing, so
let's not worry. We are too many people at home. What we have to
do is stay all together for a few days."

Sarah looked at her son with amazement and admiration. This
time, she could recognise a shadowy resemblance to David. She
began believing what Lilly had always maintained about Simon
being her father. Everything that had been happening to her
family since that fatal day, when David had been assassinated,
was incredible. Her world had been devastated and stolen
from her.

She finally simulated a poor smile, kneeled, and kissed Simon
tenderly without reserve for the first time since he was born. She
finally said, "You are right, Simon, but anyway let's enjoy these
two days, and we will be all of us home together, OK?"

Simon smiled, understanding that she trusted his analysis of the
situation. Lilly came to Simon and whispered in his right ear, "I
love you, Dad, Simon. I trust and will do everything you say." She
kissed him. It was so weird that a ten-year-old girl would call a
five-year-old "Dad."

Eric also approached him and said, "Are you supposed to be
the eldest here, and we're to listen to you?" Though he said it
jokingly, there was a little bit of resentment in it as well. He patted
Simon's head and said, "You are a smart cookie."

They all had breakfast, and after that the adults prepared for Key
West and picked up a few things. Simon asked if he could invite
his friend John, the neighbour's son, to come with them, he is not
going to school either. He was Simon's only friend, and Simon
insisted on taking him.

Sarah agreed, and she and Simon and went to the neighbour's house and rang the doorbell. A man opened the door, smiled, and said, "Good morning, Mrs Adler. Hi, Simon."

Sarah said, "Good morning, Mr Bentley. We are going to Key West, and Simon will not go without John. Can you please allow him to come with us? We are going just for two days in our camping car, my in-laws' caravan. The boys will have a great time."

He said, "Please come in. I personally have no objection, but let me ask my wife."

His wife, hearing the commotion, came out of the kitchen, saw Sarah, and said, "Hi, Sarah, how are you?" She kissed Sarah and Simon on his head.

Mr Bentley said, "Well, they are going for two days to the Keys in caravan, and Simon will not go without John. What do you say? I am sure that Sarah will take good care of him."

Mrs Bentley said, "Of course. I would be pleased to let John go." She turned to John and asked, "Do you want to go?"

John said, "Yes, Mommy, and thanks! I really want to. We will have fun."

She said, "OK, let's go and get your things ready." She said to Sarah, "I will be right back. Please sit down."

Sarah said, "No thanks. I still have to finish getting the children's things ready." To John she said, "When you are ready, come on over. We will be leaving soon enough." She shook hands with Mr Bentley, and she and Simon left.

Soon they were on their way to Key West. They tried to put aside their worries and enjoy the trip.

***

The FBI agent Jerry was about to call Bender when the latter called.

Bender said, "Hi, Jerry. Do you have something for me?"

Jerry said, "Good morning to you too. Yes, I have. OK, let's make it simple. Sarah Adler, born in Chicago to Dan and Esther Adler. She got married to David Hirsh, son of Jacob and Rachel Hirsh, born in New York, but now retired in Boca Raton, Florida. Sarah and David had three children – Eric, who is twelve years old now; Lilly, who is ten; and Simon, who is five. The husband was murdered six years ago, when the wife was pregnant with Simon. The husband died before Simon was born and didn't even know his wife was pregnant. Simon was pronounced dead at birth, but for an unknown reason, he came back to life ..." Jerry continued, relating the incidents with the FBI and the satellites and so on.

Bender listened without saying a word. Now he at least knew that the captain wasn't trying to set him up. That eased the tension he'd been feeling since yesterday. He had already imagined taking extreme action against his partner. He, who usually was so pragmatic, had become paranoid.

Jerry asked, "So does this answer all your questions?"

Bender said, "Good enough. You will get your gin as usual. Thanks, bye."

He knew now where to start. He drove to the address in Boca Raton that Jerry had given him. It took him about thirty minutes to get there. He got to know the surroundings of the house. It was a nice neighbourhood of very expensive homes. He drove slower when he passed by the number 12 home, where David's parents lived. It seemed that no one was home.

He went around the block, and once he saw that no one was looking at him, he parked. He exited the car and looked around. He saw what looked to be mostly retired people, some mowing their lawns and some just walking their dogs. To the right of the Adler's' home, a man and a woman in their forties were leaving their house. They were the Bentleys, going shopping.

Bender thought that taking care of the situation would be simple. He had not decided yet if he had to get rid of the whole family or just the kid. He still did not know how the child knew about what he'd done in the Everglades. He also didn't know if the kid would be able to recognise him that seemed impossible because it was after midnight and there was no way the kid could have recognized him in the total darkness. That was the $64,000 question. In any case, this kid and maybe his family had to be secured, so this would never come back to haunt him.

He went back to his car, drove off, and called the captain. "Hi, it's me. We have to meet soon."

The captain said, "OK. As usual?"

Bender said, "Earlier, let's make it five o'clock."

"I can't, but I can do six thirty."

"OK, see you."

Bender went back to his precinct to show himself around the office and maybe think of a strategy.

***

In Key West, the family was going around shopping and sightseeing. Lilly was sitting with John and Simon on the beach. John and Simon chatted about whales, big sharks, and barracudas. Simon and John loved fishing; they both watched

88

many documentaries about it. The conversation was more like one between two adults and not two five-year-old kids.

Simon asked, "Johnny, have you gone fishing before?"

John said, "Yes, of course. I go with my dad. He also loves it. We even go in a boat, and we catch plenty of fish."

Simon said, "I love it, but I've never gone."

"Why not come with us next time?"

At that moment the adults and Eric arrived, and they all went to eat. They were enjoying their time there. The children were happy. Eric felt a bit lonely, though. He was at a difficult age, and because of his younger brother, he couldn't bring any friends home. He loved his sister and brother, but the loss of his father had made him grow too fast. He was a young adult.

The grandparents were very compassionate and loving. They had to replace the father the children had lost. The children loved their grandparents very much. This was a great occasion to discover and know more about each other, and they did need each other. Simon was that special link that kept them all bound together.

***

The captain arrived to the bar early around six o'clock. Bender was already waiting for his arrival. The captain saw him and waved. "Hi, Bender. What was so urgent?" He sat down at his table.

Bender said, "Well, I know exactly who these people are. I called a contact at the FBI, and he gave me all the info about them."

"Are you nuts or what? Why call the FBI? You want everyone to know? I gave you the info about them."

"What you gave me was nothing, all worthless information. The guy in the FBI is good, and he is not for free." Bender proceeded to inform him who these people really were.

The captain asked, "So this child is some kind medium, how else could he have known about the everglades "?

"Something like that. Who cares? We have to get rid of all of them. I am sure that they all know. That's probably the reason that they are all hiding."

"So when do you make the move?"

Bender said, "So we'll do it Sunday night. We'll make it look like robbers got caught in stealing and shot all of them. You need to come with me; I can't do it alone."

"No way. You take one of your degenerates to do it with you and then get rid of him."

"As you wish. You don't like to dirty your hands; it's always me. OK, it will be Sunday night, and I will be there when they arrive."

The captain said, "Be careful. I know I don't have to tell you, but keep everything clean, and make it look real. Also, I am not hot about killing children. We've never done before. We are getting closer to hell, every time deeper and deeper. We have to think about stopping what we are doing. We used to be good cops, and now we are murderers."

"Now you suddenly have a conscience?" Bender asked.

"Dammit," the captain said, "are you forgetting that you and I have children? After killing these children, how will we be able to look ours in the eyes?"

"Listen, if you have another suggestion, make it now, before we make this move. I am not hot about all this, but how else can we resolve this problem?"

The captain said, "OK, we will do it this time only. I am leaving; we'll talk once it's done. Bye."

"OK, Cap, stay cool. I will take care of everything. Bye."

***

It was already Sunday; the family left Key West after lunch, around two thirty. The travel time to Boca was about four hours. They had enjoyed their time in Key West. It really had done a lot of good for the whole family, clearing their minds.

Bender arrived with his accomplice to the house around six in the evening. It was already dark, and there was no one around in the neighbouring houses, at least no one outside. This helped facilitate their job breaking into the house. It had to look like a real robbery.

With a can of foam Bender filled up the alarm box where the siren was. The foam in a matter of seconds became hard like styrofoam, which neutralised the alarm. The alarm wasn't so sophisticated; Bender had neutralised a lot more sophisticated alarms than this one. Then they cut a large circular hole into the rear glass door, near the lock. They used a diamond cutter to prevent breaking the glass.

Bender's accomplice was nicknamed "the Death" because wherever he went, someone was about to die. He was about 6 5" tall and probably in his thirties. He had grey hair cut in a short military style. He was thin and looked like a pall-bearer, dressed all in black. His face was long and thin like a knife, and his eyes were as cold as ice. He had gold caps on his two front teeth. His smile was a grin, and a big scar went from his left eye down his cheek. In other words, he was a scary vision for anyone. It was said that he had at least thirty murders to his name.

Once inside, Bender ordered the Death to go upstairs, take anything of real value, empty all drawers and closets, check

91

behind wall pictures, and look for a safe. It had to look like a break-in. As a policeman, Bender knew exactly how to make it look.

The Death went upstairs and did as ordered. Bender stayed on the ground floor. He made sure to cut the phone lines, but he did not undo or move anything yet. This way, when they came home, they wouldn't immediately call the police. He would undo the ground floor after they had killed everyone.

After forty minutes, Bender heard a car in the driveway. He immediately switched off his torch and notified the Death, by walkie-talkie, to come down and hide. They did not even bother wearing masks, because everyone in this house had to be eliminated.

They heard voices, but no one came inside. Bender did not understand why no one was coming in. Suddenly he noticed a key being introduced into the lock. Dan and Jacob entered and switched on the living room lights, followed by their wives, Eric, and Lilly. They carried bags and other things. Bender counted the people; two were missing, Sarah and Simon.

The kids were about to go upstairs when Bender and the Death came out, armed with guns, and motioned everyone not to make a sound. They all froze, especially looking at the Death. Pointing, Bender indicated they should enter the next room and said, "If anyone does anything, we will kill the children first, understood?"

They all nodded.

Outside, Sarah and Simon had returned from dropping off John. They were about to enter when Simon stopped on the spot, right before putting his foot on the first step up to the door. He whispered to Sarah, "Do not move; danger is inside the house. It's Bender, the killer cop I told you about, and someone very bad, ten times worse, is with him. Come behind me, Mom, and do not do anything. I know what to do."

Sarah said, "Let's call the police."

Simon said, "No, he holds our family hostage and will kill them for sure. I know what I am doing. Follow me."

Sarah followed him like a zombie, without even trying to make sense of what was happening. Once inside, they did not see anyone, but Simon said, "Mr Bender, you and your friend can come out. I know that you are here. Come out please."

A voice told him to close the door behind him and come to the next room. It was Bender; he showed his face after he heard the door close. Sarah and Simon went to the room where the rest of the family was detained. Sarah tried to hold Simon behind her to protect him, but Simon did not accept that and came out to the front.

The Death asked, "Is this a midget or a real child?"

Bender said, "He is a child but a very weird one, some kind of a medium. He told an officer about my involvement in a case. He has a mouth bigger than his size."

Sarah said, "Leave us alone. We will not talk to anyone, and we will forget about it. I swear. They are only children; please don't harm them."

Simon said, "Save your breath, Mom. They're not wearing masks, which means they won't leave witnesses."

Bender said, "He is smart, the kid. Move to the end of the room with your folks now; move."

Sarah and Simon moved towards the family, and they all hugged each other. Simon faced the two killers. They added silencers to their guns and pointed their guns towards the family. They chose Simon first. The ladies were crying and hiding Eric and Lilly behind them.

Simon stood in the front, staring at them. They were about to open fire without even the remotest remorse when suddenly a light came out from Simon's body. The assassins did not understand what was going on.

Bender said, "What the hell?"

The Death opened his eyes wide as if he had seen a ghost. Then the assassins saw their victims begin swirling around them. Slowly the victims' faces turned into something out of a nightmare. Their skin peeled off as they turned to skeletons.

The family could not see what the killers were seeing, so they didn't understand what was scaring the killers so much or what they were looking at, their heads swivelling from right to left and all round.

The Death said, "Stop this hocus-pocus. This is a magic trick, and he is using our minds against us."

They were prepared to shoot when Simon said, "This is no trick. Look at each other."

They turned their heads, and both screamed in terror. They began shooting at the other, and they both got killed.

Sarah asked, "What just happened here?"

The whole family was dumbfounded, not understanding what had just transpired.

Jacob said, "This is unreal. Instead of shooting at us, they shot at each other. What happened, Simon? What did you do to them?"

They were all hanging on to Simon's every word as he said, "I did not do a thing. A part of me is, in a way, from another reality. I cannot extend on that now, but it means that, being next to my other presence, their eyes were opened. They could see each other the way they really were, their ugly souls. It must have been scary. So they saw each other as horrifying monsters. From the scare they shot and killed each other."

Dan said, "It's unbelievable. If I hadn't seen it with my own eyes, I could not have believed it in a thousand years. I have to call the police now."

Sarah asked, "How can we explain what happened?"

Eric said, "We will tell the truth, and that's it." He went and hugged Simon.

Lilly kissed Simon and said, "I knew that you would protect us, Daddy." She called him Daddy without thinking about how the others were watching and listening.

Finally, David's mother asked a burning question. "Simon, are you also my son, David?"

The silence was so heavy that it could be cut with a knife. They all waited for an answer to the question that they had avoided and been apprehensive to ask for so long.

Simon did not hesitate and answered in a wise manner, "In a way, I am partly my father's son and partly him. There is something of Dad in me; I mean his personality is present most of the time. When there is a danger, he takes over and defends the family. I cannot say more than that for now."

Lilly said, "I always said it, and I was always reprimanded. But I always knew."

Sarah and the mothers were crying, not knowing what to say or do. The tears were from joy, but Simon did not say exactly that he was David. They just hugged him, no one asking more questions or saying a word.

On the phone with the police, Dan said, "Yes, my name is Dan Adler. Two people came to kill us, and they are dead." He listened to the policeman, answered the asked questions, and hung up.

Not even five minutes later, police sirens sounded, and they heard strong squeaking brakes outside their residence. There was a loud knock at the door. Jacob was there already and opened the door. Six or seven police officers stormed into the house.

One of the officers asked, "What happened? Where are the bodies?"

Dan said, "Follow me."

A lieutenant arrived at that moment and said hello to Dan and Jacob. The lieutenant and other officers followed them into the room with the two bodies lying on the floor, the assassins' eyes opened wide in terrified expressions. They had various bullet holes all over their torsos.

The lieutenant said, "Shit, it's Officer Bender; he's a cop. What the hell happened here?"

Jacob told the whole story, omitting the part about Simon. The lieutenant told an officer to call the lab team and the coroner. He then asked Jacob to excuse him for a second. He called the captain on his mobile phone. "Hi, Captain, it's me, Earl. I'm at the house of the Hirsh family. There is something very strange here. One of the two supposed robbers is – you won't believe it – a cop that we know. It's Bender, sir."

The captain for a moment was speechless. He had been sure that the lieutenant would be announcing the deaths of the whole family, but instead his two men were dead.

The lieutenant said, "Cap! Are you there, Cap?"

The captain said, "Yes, I am here. This is incredible. Are all the members of the family all right?"

"Yes, sir, and I do not understand what has happened here. It looks like the two robbers shot at each other. The other one is a known criminal – the Death. We've been looking for him for over five years."

The captain said, "I am on my way to you." He couldn't understand what had gone wrong. How would he be able to explain this situation? He was really worried about the possibility of being implicated in this incident. His heart was beating very hard. Future problems were forecasted on his agenda.

He finally arrived at the Hirsh's' residence. The police surrounded the house with yellow caution tape stating "Crime Scene." The officers saluted the captain as he entered the house. The lieutenant stepped up and said, "This way, Captain."

When they entered the room, the first person the captain saw was Sarah. "Hello again, Mme." he said. "Sorry to meet twice in such circumstances."

Sarah said, "We have nothing to do with either case. These two men were here and wanted to kill us, and we do not know why. I think they were trying to rob us and take our home; only G-d knows why." She did not tell the entire story about Simon.

In the room, the lab people were busy taking pictures and marking the spots where the bullet casings had fallen. Bender and the Death were dressed in black commando suits, but they wore no masks. It was strange for the captain to see Bender lying there, eyes wide open as if looking at the captain. His face had a frozen expression of horror, as if he had seen Satan himself.

One of the lab officers approached the captain and said, "Captain, no doubts, they shot each other; the bullets prove that theory. Can we take the corpses to the morgue?"

The captain said, "OK, go ahead." He turned to Sarah and the rest of the family and said, "One of the two men is a police officer, and it looks as if he killed the other man trying to protect you."

They were about to refute this theory when Sarah jumped in and said, "Thank G-d that he was here. It was all so fast, and we did not have time to realise what was really going on." Sarah held a hand over Simon's mouth because she knew that he would say what he had in mind. The rest of the family understood her move and approved it.

The captain said, "Since one of the men was a police officer, a special team, the police of the police, will be investigating. So please remember what we just said, and then you will just have to repeat it. OK?"

Sarah nodded. The captain told all the officers to pack up and leave. Then he turned to Sarah and asked, "By the way, has anything been stolen? I see that on the upper floor various things were packed to be taken."

Sarah said, "I don't think so. I don't think they … he had time to take anything, Captain."

The captain said, "I'll need you to make a statement. Can you come to my office tomorrow? Or maybe it would be better for me to come here, so I won't impose this on you a second time this week."

"That will be fine, thank you."

"Ten in the morning OK for you?"

"Yes."

The captain said, "Then I will see you tomorrow. Bye." He turned around and left. All the crew and police officers had left already.

All the family gathered in the living room. Dan was the first one to speak. "This is all bull. They were both murderers and tried to kill us, period."

Sarah said, "If we'd said that, he would have to explain why they shot each other. No, it's better this way."

Simon said, "You are all wrong. He is the boss, and he is the one that ordered them to kill all of us."

They all looked at him, stupefied and horrified by this shocking new information.

Simon continued, "The captain has a gang infiltrated in the police force. They are crooks and killers; nothing will stop them from getting what they want." Simon was again speaking like an adult and had a very serious expression on his face.

Sarah asked, "What are we going to do?"

Jacob said, "Let's play his game and see what happens."

Dan said, "You are right, Jacob. We will have to be very careful. I am almost positive that he might try again to get rid of us."

Simon said, "I will be very attentive to our situation. We will see then."

Sarah said, "It's already past midnight. Let's go to sleep. We've had more than enough emotions for the day. Tomorrow will be another day. Goodnight, all."

***

As the captain left the house, he thought that this time the problem was coming too close to him. He'd never believed that this kid would cause him so many problems. He kept seeing Bender's dead face. Bender had been in so many dangerous situations and always gotten away alive, mostly against drug or arms dealers. Now, against a five-year-old kid, he and the dangerous criminal the Death had ended up dead. How was this possible?

Now he would have the inspection of the police of the police on his back. He hoped that Sarah would say what he'd suggested to the inspectors that would be there for sure tomorrow. He felt trapped with no one to talk to. He did not know Bender's contact at the FBI.

He thought, *Maybe I should disappear. I have over $7 million. Maybe I should go to Brazil, where there is no extradition. How will I explain this to my wife? My daughter is sixteen years old. She will not take it rationally. She won't want to leave all her friends, and my wife won't leave her parents; I'm 100 per cent sure about that.*

Tomorrow he would be interrogated, and he would deny everything. They had no direct proof of his involvement. He had no choice but to wait, and then he would decide what to do. He did not have the guts to go against this family again. The kid must be the Devil. He remembered how the pervert at the movie theatre had been burned just by looking at the kid. Even though there was no proof, he knew that the boy had done it. And how else had he found out about Bender? He must be one of Satan's offspring.

The captain was shivering and clenching his teeth from fright. For the first time in his life he was really scared. He was positive this kid was not human. He went to a bar and tried to drown his worries in a bottle of whisky.

***

At eight o'clock the next morning, Sarah was already up. She decided not to send the children to school. She knew that the captain was supposed to come for the statement. Maybe she would send the children away with their grandmothers to go shopping; this would prevent Simon from saying things that would cause more problems than they already had.

She went upstairs and woke Eric and Lilly first. Then she went to Simon's room. She opened the shades, turned towards Simon, and almost screamed. Simon's face was now identical to David's.

Oh my G-d, no, it's not possible, Sarah thought. Simon was still asleep. The lines of his face had completely changed. He even looked a little older. How could this be possible? How could she forget the face, this face that she loved so much and that she missed so much? Simon's had always looked so much like David's, but now it was an exact copy. How could this happen overnight?

She took him to the shower and dressed him. When she came down with him, the rest of the family was having breakfast. They all froze in what they were doing, even Eric and Lilly, when they saw Simon. They even stopped chewing their food.

David's parents had tears in their eyes, and both said, "Oh my G-d!"

Sarah's parents couldn't utter a single word, but their expression said everything.

Lilly said, "He looks so much like Daddy. What happened to you, Simon?"

Simon said, "Nothing, why?"

Lilly said, "Look at yourself in the mirror."

Simon went to the dining room to look in the mirror, came back, and said, "I don't see anything new! What am I supposed to see?"

Sarah said, "Nothing, my love, just nothing. Sit down and have breakfast."

They all looked at each other without uttering a single word. Sarah finally broke the silence and said, "The captain will be here soon. Could you ladies take the kids for a ride? And Dad and Jacob can stay with me? I don't want Simon to be here when this guy comes in."

Sarah's mother said, "OK, no problem. We will go after breakfast."

At that moment, the doorbell rang. They all looked at each other. As Jacob went to open the door, Sarah said, "He is a little early. Let's finish and go get ready. The grandmas will take you kids out."

Jacob opened the door to reveal three gentlemen in suits. They showed their badges; they were from the FBI. The tallest spoke first. "Agent Walker from the FBI. I would like to speak with Mrs Sarah Hirsh, sir."

Jacob said, "That's my daughter-in-law. Please come in."

Once the three men were inside, Jacob called Sarah. She came out, followed by her father. The three FBI men came towards her, and Agent Walker introduced himself and his colleagues, Agent Heston and Agent Johnson.

Sarah said, "FBI? I was expecting a police captain to take our statement of the robbery. Please take a seat." As the agents sat down in the living room, she asked, "Can I offer you coffee or juice?"

They nodded in the affirmative, and Agent Walker said, "Yes, we know the captain was supposed to come, but we are here because there has been some suspicious activity. When we heard that a police officer had been killed, we put your name in the computer, and we noticed that an FBI agent had recently requested information about you and your family."

He continued, "When we questioned the officer, he confessed that an acquaintance, a policeman by the name of Bender, had contacted him three days ago wanting to know everything about all of you. As Bender was the police officer killed in your house, we immediately came here, to hear directly from you all what happened. So, if you don't mind, we will interrogate each of you, separately."

Sarah said, "But we already told the police everything."

Walker said, "I understand, but now it is officially the Bureau's case, since our databank was involved and a policeman is dead. So we are taking over."

Dan said, "I don't see a problem."

Sarah said, "OK, whenever you are ready." She left momentarily and returned with the agents' drinks.

Walker said, "One of us will speak to each of you, including the children."

So each agent took one family member. Sarah was in the living room, Jack in the dining room, and Dan in the kitchen. Walker was interrogating Sarah.

He said, "Mrs Hirsh, the police explained about the so-called robbery, but I want to know if the two were accomplices or if one of them tried to protect you and shot the other one. Please, you have to tell me the whole truth, and know that we already have a very good picture of what happened."

Sarah said, "Well, the police said that it looked like Officer Bender tried to help us, but that couldn't be further from the truth. He was the one that gave the orders and that planned to kill us. We never met him before yesterday. I do not know why they wanted to kill us." She told the story from the movie theatre and how the man had gotten burned and then, to the police station for the statement until today.

Sarah, Dan, and Jacob were done with the questioning, and then it was the grandmothers' and Eric's turn. Thirty minutes later they were done. Now it was time for Lilly's and Simon's interrogations. The family was afraid of what Simon would say. The problem was that no one could dictate his words.

Agent Walker said, "Hi, Simon. My name is Walker, and I am from the FBI. How are you, son?"

"I am not your son!" Simon said.

"Sorry, I did not mean it in that context; it's just an expression."

"I don't understand why people say things they don't mean."

Agent Walker felt embarrassed and did not know how to continue the conversation. This child was a bit strange, and even though he was just five years old, he spoke like an adult. Walker could swear that Simon's eyes were penetrating his subconscious. It was hard to sustain Simon's eyes.

Agent Walker finally said, "Well, let's begin with what has happened last night."

Simon said, "This was not a robbery. They came to kill all of us."

"Why would they want to kill you? Did you know them?"

"No, but I knew everything about their murders."

Agent Walker asked, "But how can you know things you haven't seen?"

"I just know things," Simon said. "Like your wife's name is July, she is thirty-five years old, and she is pregnant."

Agent Walker was stunned. How could he know that? But July wasn't pregnant, and he said so.

Simon said, "Call her. She is at the doctor's office finding out that she is pregnant."

Walker instinctively picked up his mobile phone and walked away, calling his wife. Sarah, even though she was not next to Simon, could hear what he and Agent Walker were saying loud and clear. She was worried about the extent of where this conversation was going.

Agent Walker came back and looked at Simon in a very strange way. With a half-smile he said, "Simon, how can you know all this? Even my wife had just found out when I called. She couldn't believe that I knew about it. I did not tell her how I found out. You are really incredible. Thank you very much about my news, but now, how did Officer Bender find out you knew about the murders?"

Simon said, "The captain of police told him; he was their boss."

Now Walker did not doubt Simon's statement. This was the missing information that gave sense to the whole story. The captain was the boss, and he, Bender, and his other acolytes were killing and stealing with impunity. Worst of all, they were doing it under the protection of their badges, so no one dared go against them. Now the problem was to prove it.

Simon read Walker's mind and understood his dilemma. He said, "Go to 112 North West and 63rd Avenue. He has a storage unit, number 1728. It's under the name of Gorge Stanislaw. You will find money, drugs, documents, and much more in there. You'll find everything you need to catch this criminal."

Agent Walker said, "It sounds so incredible, but you seem to know all these things, and you've proved that you are very special."

At that moment, the doorbell rang. Jacob went and opened the door. To the surprise of all present, it was the police captain. Everyone looked at him. Seeing the FBI agents, the captain became pale. Jacob invited him in. He entered but felt very uneasy. He probably felt something bad for him in the air.

The captain said, "Good morning to you all. I was supposed to meet Sarah this morning. Is it a bad time?"

Agent Walker said, "Come in, Captain; you arrived at a good time."

One of the other agents came behind him and took his weapon.

The captain said, "What the hell!"

"Save your breath," Agent Walker said. "We know everything about you, Bender, and company. When I say everything, I mean everything."

The third agent pointed his gun at the captain while the other handcuffed him.

"We will be leaving you all now," Agent Walker said. "Mrs Hirsh, thanks for everything. We will be in touch very soon. Bye."

The captain looked at Sarah first and then Simon with a murderous look. The two agents pushed him out, and Walker followed, smiling and winking at Simon.

Once they had left, Sarah hugged Simon and kissed him warmly. "Oh, Simon, you are so special," she said. "You surprise us all the time. I can't say that we are ever bored with you. Why can't you just avoid telling everything you know?"

Simon said, "You have to understand that I cannot lie. I am connected to a different reality where lying is not an existing expression or thought. I am connected to two different realities: Simon to this one and David to the other."

They all looked at each other. If they had doubts about him being David before, they no longer did now. Lilly was hectic, excited that everyone now knew that she was not crazy. She and Eric lifted Simon from the ground and kissed him. Eric hadn't smiled or expressed himself this way in a long time.

Dan said, "I hope that now things will cool off. It was great that in five years we did not have any problems until now. Can I count on you, Simon, for no more surprises?"

Simon said, "I cannot promise a thing. It's not me that decides but the situation or the people I meet. They are the cause, and I am the remedy. When the cause is present near me, then the remedy is activated. That's the way it works, Grandpa."

Sarah's mom asked, "What are we supposed to do now, just wait for more trouble? Or should we go to Chicago?"

Sarah said, "We have to stay here until the FBI tells us that we are OK to leave. They have to be sure that we do not have any other criminals looking for us."

***

The FBI took the captain to their office for interrogation. They found the box with over $7 million, 50 kilos of cocaine, and 35 kilos of pure heroine inside. There were also weapons, false court orders, and much, much more. It was all the proof they needed, just as Simon had said.

The FBI assistant director, arrived and entered the conference office where Walker and seven more agents were discussing Simon and his family. They stopped talking when Chief Edwards entered the room.

Chief Edwards asked, "So, do I have to congratulate you, Walker?"

Agent Walker said, "I wish that it was me that solved the murders. You will probably laugh, but it was a five-year-old kid that did." He told Chief Edwards everything that had transpired and about the kid's powers and how he'd known about July's pregnancy and everything else.

Chief Edwards said, "Well, if that is so, we don't need the FBI or police. Are you under some kind of influence or what?" He laughed loudly and said, "Let's be serious. What really happened?"

Agent Walker said, "Sir, you can ask the other two that came with me."

Chief Edwards looked at the others, and they nodded in the affirmative. One of them said, "Sir, it was real serious. This kid is something else! I was afraid that he would say something to me. Chief Edwards said, "I can't believe what I'm hearing. Bring me this child as soon as possible. I want you all to continue the investigation on those crooked cops. Don't wait for the child to solve all the cases." He again broke out in a loud, hysteric laugh and left the room.

Agent Walker was furious and embarrassed because most of his colleagues imitated their boss in making fun of him. The meeting ended on the same tone.

***

At the house the family was relaxing a bit after their hectic day. Sarah was looking at Simon in admiration. He was the man of the house in a way. He'd handled the situation better than all of them together. The more she looked at him, the more she saw David in miniature.

Dan said, "Let's go out for dinner."

Jacob said, "Great idea! Let's go and clear our minds."

Sarah said, "OK, how about Chinese?"

They all agreed, but Simon said that he was not hungry.

Jacob said, "Don't worry; you will become hungry once we are there."

They all departed for dinner.

The Next Morning

The phone rang at nine o'clock the next morning. The family had already had breakfast, and the children were about to go to school. Sarah picked up the phone and said, "Hello?"

"Hello, Mrs Hirsh, it's Agent Walker. Is this a bad time?"

"Good morning," Sarah said. "No, it's OK; the children are ready to go to school."

Agent Walker said, "Well, it's about my boss. It is imperative that you and Simon come to our office this morning. He wants to meet the two of you."

"What else is happening?"

"Nothing new. He just wants to hear all about this matter directly from Simon. You know, he couldn't believe what I told him about what had happened. I am really sorry and upset that he doesn't believe me. The truth is that I hardly believe myself, so it's no wonder he doesn't believe me."

"But could this cause us trouble?"

"No, of course not," Agent Walker said.

"So when should we be there?"

"I will come to pick you up at 11 a.m. Is that OK with you?"

"Yes, see you then," Sarah said and hung up.

Sarah explained the conversation to the grandparents. They did not like it so much, but they had no other choice. Lilly and Eric left for school, accompanied by the grandparents. Sarah got ready and also dressed Simon accordingly. Sarah thought this Agent Walker seemed to be a nice guy. He was very polite and gentle.

The doorbell rang at 11 a.m. sharp. Sarah and Simon were ready. She opened the door, and there Agent Walker was. He was a bit embarrassed, as he really admired Sarah and thought she was a really beautiful women.

"Good morning, Miss Sarah," he said.

"Good morning, Agent Walker," Sarah replied.

"Please let us go; the chief is waiting for us."

They drove off towards the local FBI head office in Florida. It took them twenty minutes to get there. Once they arrived, Walker accompanied Sarah and Simon to the chief's office. Walker invited Sarah and Simon to take a seat in the conference room. "I will go and notify the boss, and I will be right back." He turned around and left the room.

Sarah smiled at Simon and said, "Be yourself, my darling; I trust you 100 per cent."

Simon smiled back and said, "Do not worry, Sarah; I know exactly what to say and do."

Sarah was not shocked that Simon called her by her name and not Mommy. She understood that it was David speaking. She caressed his face and hair and smiled back at him.

Someone cleared his throat behind them, and they both stood up and turned towards the door. There was a tall, heavy built white man, around 6′ 7″, with grey hair and blue eyes. He looked to be in his fifties and had very large hands. He wore a very severe expression but made every effort to sound nice and was smiling at them.

Agent Walker stood beside the man and said, "Chief, this is Mrs Hirsh, and this is Simon."

The chief shook Sarah's hand and then Simon's. "Madam, it's a pleasure, and you are Simon; you are famous here. Please, take a seat." They all sat down, and the chief asked, "Can I offer you something to drink? Or anything else?"

Sarah said, "Water will be fine, thanks." Simon did not want anything.

The chief called to have someone bring coffee and water. He then turned towards Sarah and asked, "Mrs Hirsh, do you mind if I address Simon directly?"

"Please do," Sarah said, looking at Simon for his approval.

Simon said almost immediately, "I know, sir, that you have doubts about this whole matter. I know that you have been divorced from your wife, Angela, for three years and also that you lost your mother last month." The chief couldn't believe his ears. Simon continued, "You have a daughter named Alina. She is five years old. You should take her to a very good gynaecologist. She has a problem with her ovaries. If taken care of now, she will have no problems later; if not, later in life she won't be able to have children."

The chief was frozen; he couldn't utter a word. Everything Simon had said about his situation and the names was correct, but the chief had had no clue about Alina's health problem. He finally said, "This is really something. It is hard to believe what I have heard just now. With your permission, I will call my wife and tell her to go immediately to see a specialist."

He picked up his mobile phone, dialled, and left the room for a moment.

Agent Walker was smiling, happy to see his boss so confused and shocked by what he'd heard. Now the chief would believe him and would not make fun of him.

Ten minutes later, the chief came back and said, "I am really sorry, but I had to explain to my ex-wife about Alina and what the doctor should check. Simon, you are beyond me entirely. Walker, I'm sorry if I made fun of you. I know that if I tell my superiors about this, they will think that I've lost it."

There were a few minutes of silence, and suddenly Simon spoke again. "Sir, you will get back together with your wife soon. Your daughter's future is good; they have an appointment in two hours, with Dr Levy. She will be in good hands."

Simon didn't stop amazing the chief.

Simon then said, "I will also tell you something probably more important. I know that you are all looking for Salim el-Maliki. He is responsible for many terrorist attacks against Americans around the world."

The chief and Walker looked at each other. They knew exactly who this terrorist was. There was a $50 million bounty on his head, dead or alive. He was number two on the international most-wanted list.

Simon continued, "You can find him in Vancouver, Canada. He is there with five known terrorists." Simon listed the other terrorists' names. "They are in a private villa at 324 bis Duran Street. They have recently arrived from Iran. They have a violent virus which makes Ebola look like a simple cold. They're keeping it in a small stainless steel container which they are hiding inside a guitar."

The chief asked, "Are you sure about this, Simon? These are very serious accusations."

Simon said, "They will try to contaminate various train stations. I will give you a list of which ones. This virus will spread at a very fast rate, about 1,000 infected per minute."

The chief asked, "What are you saying? When will this attack happen? Are you sure, Simon?"

Agent Walker asked, "Are you sure that they came from Iran?"

Simon said, "Yes, I am as sure as I am here with you. Iran is attacking the world by proxies. They are waging war on the whole planet without anyone raising an eyebrow. Iran is using all the extremists; they are the ones to choose the targets and provide the financing. They are distributing hundreds of millions of dollars to terrorist chiefs, who then send their fanatics on missions. They have similar plans against most of Europe, Russia, China, the Philippines, Australia, and many more places. Their motto is to kill as many infidels as possible."

The chief asked, "But if you know all this, why have you not said anything before?"

"I only discover these things when I meet a person who has a worry or a problem. Then I know about everything that person touches and about the information that person deals with. Then I have the response or the solution for it. So when I met you an hour ago, I then knew everything that you are in touch with."

The chief said, "Walker, please take Mrs Hirsh and Simon for lunch at the cafeteria. I will join you as soon as possible. I have to discuss this information with my superiors."

Agent Walker stood up and said, "Please follow me; we will go to the cafeteria now."

Simon said to the chief, "Sir, you are distracted from the source of the danger. These terrorists are only a small part of this war. Your real enemy is Iran and radical Islam, but most of the world is looking the other way. What is wrong with all of you?" He did not wait for an answer and followed his mother and Agent Walker.

They left the room, leaving the chief perplexed and not knowing what to say or how to handle this situation. He picked up the phone and asked his secretary to call the director of the FBI in Washington, DC. The secretary got the director on the phone and then said, "Sir, I have Mr Fleming on the line."

The chief said, "Hi, boss. You, Mr Tanner from the CIA, and I have to meet in Langley immediately. And then after our first meeting we need to meet with the secretary of state. It is imperative that we maintain full secrecy about this meeting. It's a must, sir."

Mr Fleming said, "OK, if it is so important, come to Washington. I will notify Tanner. Come as soon as you can. Bye."

Sarah, Simon, and Agent Walker were sitting in the cafeteria when the chief arrived. He ordered a sandwich and sat at their table. He then said, "Mrs Hirsh, I spoke to my superiors. What your son has told us is very serious and has put the bosses of the FBI, CIA, and Homeland Security on full alert."

Seeing the gravity of the situation and the chief's pale face, which indicated his worry, Sarah grew worried herself. "Is there something that we can do to help?" she asked.

The chief said, "Yes, there is. I will not hide it from you: I need you and Simon to come with me to Washington to meet my superiors."

For a few seconds, the silence was so thick you could cut it with a knife. They all looked at each other. Sarah broke the silence. "But how? When?"

The chief said, "We would leave in our private plane in ten minutes. They expect us in a couple of hours. I am afraid that if Simon does not meet the bosses, they will never take me seriously."

Sarah said, "But my family will be worried. I have to call them and explain."

The chief said, "I am sorry, but you cannot tell them what we are doing or where we are going; it's a matter of national security. You can say that we will be in a long meeting and that we are going to North Carolina and that it is very important, period."

Sarah asked, "Can I use your phone to call my parents and in-laws and to talk to my children?"

"Of course," the chief said, "but remember the need for censorship of this extremely dangerous situation. Now, we have to hurry; a car is waiting to take us to a private airport, where the FBI plane is waiting and ready to go."

Sarah nodded, picked up the phone, and dialled the house in Boca Raton. After three rings, Jacob picked up the phone and said, "Hello?"

Sarah said, "Hi, Jacob; it's Sarah. Please put the speaker on, so I won't have to repeat myself."

"Go ahead, Sarah; everyone is listening to you."

"Hi, everyone! Simon and I will probably be going to Washington for reasons I cannot explain"

Dan asked, "Are you sure that Simon and you are OK?"

"Yes, we are. Do not worry; we are OK. We cannot talk on the phone, but I will explain when we come back. Eric, Lilly, are you there?"

Eric said, "Yes, Mom, we are here."

Lilly said, "Hi, Mommy."

Walker indicated To Sarah that she had to hurry, so she said, "OK, everyone, we have to go. Bye! Love you, guys." She finally hung up, and she and Simon followed Walker; the chief had already left for the car.

Once in the car, they departed immediately to the airport. After forty-five minutes they arrived at a small airport, where a jet was waiting for them. They all exited the car and went up the plane.

Simon said, "Stop. Send this pilot to a hospital. He has a respiratory problem. When the plane reaches 5,000 feet, he will feel very bad and have difficulty breathing. Get another pilot."

Without asking any questions the chief spoke to the pilot and asked to get another pilot immediately. He ordered the pilot to go to the hospital to be checked for respiratory issues.

No one dared to ask questions, and the pilot's second called and requested a pilot replacement. They were lucky; one was waiting for another client. He was requisitioned for national security, and he could not refuse. He asked the office to notify the clients and to get another pilot.

The pilots, Sarah, Simon, and the FBI guys boarded the plane. They taxied down the runway, and the plane lifted off. Now they were on the way.

The chief was looking at Simon and thinking about how this child had put everyone in combat preparation. It was so incredible that it had to be seen to be believe. He imagined how his superiors would take it. He was dying to see their faces.

Simon fell asleep, and the chief thought, *My G-d, I swear that his face has changed; I am positive. Before he looked so serious for a child his age, and now he looks like an angel, the way a child should look.* He couldn't take his eyes off him.

Sarah was chatting with Walker about the police captain.

Agent Walker said, "You know, this morning he attempted to commit suicide. The case against him is tight and practically sealed. He is overwhelmed by all the witnesses and evidence. There's enough to take him away for a very long time".

Sarah said, "I hope that he doesn't have a way to take revenge against us."

"He is in solitary confinement, and no one can approach or talk to him. No one will be able to save him."

"I feel a bit guilty for what is happening to him."

"On the contrary, Simon is a hero. He got rid of them single-handedly. I still don't understand how he managed to have them shoot each other. This is a mystery for all of us. I hope that one day Simon will reveal his secrets."

The phone rang, and the chief picked it up. It was his secretary. She said, "Boss, your wife is on the line; she wants to talk to you, sir."

The chief said, "Go ahead and put her through."

His wife said, "My love, Dr Levy says that the doctor who made Alina's diagnosis must be a genius. He is next to me, and he says that no one would have found it until she tried to have a child. This doctor is ahead of our time. He should be the one to operate on her. Dr Levy is asking about his name?"

The chief said, "OK, good, but I cannot talk now, darling. We will talk later. I will call you tonight after my meetings. Bye, love." He hung up.

He relayed his conversation to Sarah and Walker and said to Sarah, "Your son is a real genius. He is something else, just incredible."

"I think that Simon can cure her when we come back," Sarah said and explained about the other various cases.

Two and a half hours later, they were about to land. Simon was still asleep. Sarah kissed him gently and said, "Wake up, my darling; we are almost there."

He opened his eyes and smiled. "Hi, Mom!" It was Simon that was talking, not David.

117

The chief said, "Hello, Simon. Slept well?" Simon nodded, and the chief asked, "Simon, do you think that you can possibly cure my daughter, Alina?"

"Possibly, when I see her," Simon said with a smile.

The chief said, "Buckle up. We are landing in two minutes."

The plane landed safely. Two black Chevy 4x4s were waiting at the end of the runway. The four came down from the plane and walked towards the cars. Two agents dressed in grey suits stood next to each of the cars. They shook hands with Walker and then the chief and nodded to Sarah. The chief went in one of the vehicles, and Walker, Sarah, and Simon got in the second vehicle. They departed quickly to the FBI head office.

They soon arrived at the tall glass building with "The Federal Bureau of Investigation" in very large bronze letters over the entrance. They entered the building. Visitor tags were ready for Sarah and Simon. They pinned the tags to their jackets and went through a metal detector gate. They took the elevator to the fourteenth floor. The conference room was just across from the elevator.

They entered, and no one was there. The chief said, "Walker, please have them take a seat, and I will notify the boss. I will be right back. See if they want anything." He left.

Agent Walker said, "Please take a seat over there. Simon, next to your mother." They did, and Walker said, "Great. Would you like something to drink? Or anything else?"

Sarah said, "Coffee for me and a hot cocoa for Simon, thank you."

Agent Walker made a call from the phone on the table and requested the drinks. At that moment, the door opened, and three men and two women entered the conference room. One was the chief. Sarah and Simon stood up, and the chief made the introductions.

The chief said, "Mrs Hirsh, this is Mr Tanner, the head of the CIA." Mr Tanner was a bold-looking man in his fifties. He wore heavy glasses and had a mole in the left corner of his nose. He was a little man, about 5′ 8″, and a little heavy for his height.

"Mr Fleming is our boss, the head of the FBI," the chief continued. Mr Fleming was a handsome older man who looked very distinguished. He wore very light glasses and a black suit. He was probably in his mid sixties and was thin with grey hair. He was a retired general.

Gesturing to one of the ladies, the chief said, "This is Mrs Sullivan. She is the CIA representative at the White House." She was a gorgeous blonde in her forties. She had proud breasts and was petite, about 5′ 6″, and very well built. She smiled, showing her very nice white teeth that could be out of a TV advertisement.

Introducing the last woman, the chief said, "This is Mrs Hastings. She is our attaché at the White House. Both she and Mrs Sullivan are in direct contact with the president." Mrs Hastings was in her fifties and quite tall for a woman, probably 6′ 2″. She was built like a man, had wide shoulders, and was not pretty. Her facial expression was too serious, and that made her look less pretty.

They all shook hands with Sarah and Simon. Some stroked Simon's head. He showed clearly that he did not appreciate that. After they finished the introductions, Mr Fleming suggested they all sit.

He said, "Well, I've read the chief's report. All this sounds incredible. I understand that Simon has special powers of all sorts and that he has just detected a terrorist plot in Canada that is directed towards our country."

Without being invited to do so, Simon stood up. They all looked surprised that this child seemed so serious and serene. Simon said, "I can feel that you have doubts about me. Let me dissipate these doubts. I'll begin with you, Mrs Hastings. You had breakfast this morning with the president; you had scrambled eggs, toast, orange juice, and a blueberry muffin. Simon continued "At 7.45 a.m. the secretary of state joined both of you. The first subject of conversation was Honduras, then the threat from Canada, and then a mockery about me." They looked at him, how could Simon had know about the secret meeting this early morning

Mrs Hastings choked and looked at Simon as if he were an extraterrestrial. Walker and the chief were smiling.

Simon continued, "I can tell you that the president has a cancerous mole on his lower back, a virulent one. He will have to take it off in two weeks exactly, not before and not after."

Fleming asked, "But how can you know all this? And it is so precise. We need precision; this could help with our national security."

Sarah said, "If I may? Simon is a very special child. I am sure that you already know that he was born dead. Hours later, a miracle happened, and he revived. After his birth, all the people around him in the hospital were healed, even visitors. So after we left the hospital, Simon's paediatrician came to our home and suggested we bring Simon to the hospital, so he could help the ill."

Everyone was hanging on to Sarah's every word, completely absorbed. She continued, "The next day, I took Simon, who was a month old, to the hospital. All seemed to be working great when suddenly many deaths were reported at the hospital. The CDC came and quarantined the hospital. After many hours of checking all the deaths, they found no viruses or contagions of any kind. All the deaths seemed to be of natural causes."

Tanner said, "No one has explained those deaths? Simon, can you tell us something about it? Or you, Mrs Hirsh?"

Simon answered without hesitating, "As I bring healing to innocent people, I also can cause death to criminals or bad people that have done repulsive things, like paedophiles and people that beat the elderly. It has to be something cruel and not tolerable by anyone. I am not the one that does it; it's something that surrounds me and that works both ways. I do not wish nor do anything to trigger it. I cannot lie."

Tanner said, "I see. Thank you for your sincerity. Would you and your mother agree to help us, so we can help our country?"

Sarah asked, "What do you mean by that? What does that involve?"

Tanner said, "We will need you to move to Washington for a while. Do you agree, Fleming?" Fleming nodded in agreement.

Sarah said, "But we have a family! I have my two other children, my parents, and my in-laws!"

Fleming said, "Do not worry; we will get you a large house that can hold all of you very comfortably."

Sarah said, "But I can't decide for them."

Tanner said, "We will convince them of the importance of this situation. All of you are Americans, and you have duties to your country, as we all do."

"I understand," Sarah said, "and yes, we will do everything to be of help. But you have to appreciate that I cannot answer for them. I am sure that my parents are very patriotic."

Fleming said, "I can send for them and bring them here so it will be easier to discuss it. Please call them and let them know, without giving too much information, that I will have one of our field agents go and pick them up."

Sarah said, "All right, I will call now and—"

Simon interrupted, "There have been radical changes in the terrorists' plans. They are going to infect themselves with the virus, and each one will travel to a different destination." Simon seemed to be feeling a great pressure. His eyes for a split second turned blood red. They were all looking at him, and Sarah was very worried.

Tanner, unable to contain his impatient, asked, "What else?"

Fleming was more diplomatic. "Simon, can you tell us more? Are you OK?"

Simon seemed to come back to himself. He looked at all those present and said, "They will leave early tomorrow morning. Now that they are the virus carriers, you cannot arrest them or even shoot them. The only option left is to surround their house now with troops. The troops will have to wear chemical suits. You will then need to burn the house from all sides, without notification. The house will have to burn at 2000° Fahrenheit for a full hour. It sounds dramatic, but the other options are no longer viable."

Tanner said, "That will create a problem with the Canadian government, and we won't have time to explain."

Fleming said, "We will also have to evacuate the surrounding houses."

"There is another way," Simon said. "You can take me there. I think I can do something."

"But what happens if you can't?" Tanner asked.

Fleming said, "Then we should be ready for plan A."

Mrs Hastings said, "I will go and notify the president so he can call the Canadian prime minister for his approval."

Simon said, "Be careful. The prime minister needs to know that two of his cabinet ministers, Mr Pujol and Mr Barbieri, are not especially good Canadian citizen and have many ties with terrorist organisations and do launder money for them."

Tanner said, "This we know. Special crews will be ready as soon that I leave this office. So, Mrs Hirsh, please make your call to your family."

Fleming said, "Yes, we will send agents to pick them up. Is it OK that we take Simon with us?"

Sarah said, "But he is only five years old. I cannot leave him by himself."

They all looked at each other. Fleming shrugged his shoulders and said, "In this case, yes, you are right. We keep forgetting that he is a child after all. You can come with us."

They all stood up and began leaving the room. The situation looked so ridiculous: Simon, a five-year-old child, was the boss, and the most powerful people on earth were under his orders. It really looked comic.

Sarah picked up the phone and dialled. It rang three times until Jacob answered. She said, "Agents are coming to pick you all up to join us here. I have to go. Once we're all here, we will discuss." Walker indicated that she had to end the conversation, and she did so.

Sarah and Simon followed Agent Walker out of the building. Three cars were waiting. They got in and went to the airport. They took a different plane, which was already on the tarmac. The US government notified the prime minister of Canada about the arrival of the US team and asked him to assemble all the necessary help for a very secret operation that would be revealed to the Canadian special team. The motto was "Of the highest urgency and secrecy." The Canadian government chose commandos from the top secret service and put them at the service of the US team, directed by Mr Fleming.

When the plane landed in a military airport just outside Vancouver, ten Canadian commandos were waiting at the end of the runway. Two were in civilian clothes, probably secret service. The plane taxied up to the point where the troops were waiting. Finally, the plane stopped. Mr Fleming was the first one to come out, followed by Tanner and about twelve FBI agents dressed in military uniforms. Sarah, Simon, and Agent Walker were the last to come out. Fleming had previously given strict instructions not to say anything about Sarah and son.

The American troops were presented to their Canadian counterparts. The man that seemed to be the Canadians' boss said, "Mr Fleming, I presume?"

Mr Fleming said, "Hi, good afternoon. You are probably Mr Cummings!"

"Yes, I am. Welcome. We have a conference room waiting for us inside. That is the general's headquarters. Please follow me."

They did. Once inside, introductions were made. When it was Sarah's turn, Fleming said, "Mrs Hirsh and her son Simon." They all sat down. It was 8 p.m.

Cummings said, "Mr Fleming, can you explain what this is all about and why so much secrecy and urgency? And why are this lady and child here? With all due respect, Madam."

Fleming said, "Very pertinent questions, but before I answer them, I need all present to dispose their mobile phones without exception, including us bosses."

One by one everyone stood up, took an envelope that Walker had brought, wrote his or her name on it, and put his or her phone inside. Walker supervised.

Cummings said, "I concede that you have aroused my curiosity. You have my full and undivided attention."

"OK, this is the situation," Fleming said, and he explained the whole situation. When he finished, the silence was total. Those gathered could have heard a fly.

Cummings said, "I understand now the whys and the gravity. We are ready when you are. Here are the maps you requested. You haven't explained about this woman and her son."

"She and her son were witnesses and gave us a description of the chief of the terrorists, and they will recognise him if necessary," Fleming said.

Flemings spread the map. He handed Cummings a marker and a sheet of paper with the address of the terrorists' house and asked him to mark the address on the map. Cummings marked the house in question and said, "Here it is. What now?"

Fleming said, "We will divide into four groups, to surround the house hermetically. Do you have the necessary equipment? The fire cannons?"

"Yes, everything is ready," Cummings said. "We will have two per van. These create very high temperatures, up to 2500° Fahrenheit. They will reduce anything to dust."

Fleming said, "OK, I will keep the civilians with me in my bulletproof truck. So let's all go."

Everyone stood up and got ready to leave. The crews that were supposed to carry the fire cannons all wore chemical suits. Ten minutes later, everyone was ready. Each crew was made of six people. Two in each group had the special cannons, and the others had heavy weaponry that carried special napalm ammunitions.

Fleming took just Agent Walker, Sarah, and Simon. Walker took the driver's seat, and Cummings' van took the lead of the convoy, and Fleming's van closed it. The heavy convoy was on the way.

It was quite cold outside. There weren't many people out on the street, just a passer-by here and there. They arrived. Each command car had only one walkie-talkie. They took positions surrounding the terrorists' house, without headlights.

Walker parked on a spot between two trees, about 100 feet from the suspected house. Fleming turned and looked at Simon and asked, "So, Simon, what can you tell me?"

Simon said, "They are all here. I need to get out of the car to do what I have to do."

Fleming picked up his radio and said, "OK, everyone, it is 23:15 hours. At 23:30 we will begin; be ready." Then he said to Simon, "Go ahead and try to do whatever you can. You have fifteen minutes."

Cummings said, "We've checked by thermo, and six are inside. We will be ready."

Simon opened the car door and stepped out. He stood still in front of the car, out of sight from the commandos. He raised his arms straight in front of him and stayed like a marble statue for three minutes.

To Sarah, Fleming, and Walker, the minutes became like hours. Nothing seemed to be happening, and for a moment they thought that nothing would happen. Then suddenly, out of nowhere, a giant column of fire came from above and fell on the suspected house as another column rose from within the ground of the house. It was terrifying. Simon was sweating, and his whole body was shaking. Fleming and Walker could not believe their eyes. Sarah was crying and got worried about Simon, seeing him this way. She tried to get out, but Walker stopped her.

Cummings radioed, "What the hell! What was that? Who did that? It did not come from us!"

The house vanished, all in ashes. Simon dropped his arms, and there was no more fire.

Fleming said, "This is incredible." He opened the car door and rushed towards Simon. "Simon, what you did here is incredible. Bravo!" He lifted Simon from the ground and kissed him from the emotion. He wasn't used to kissing even his own child very often. He got in the car, and Simon sat with Sarah. She held him tight against her, crying. He was covered in sweat.

People began coming out of their homes. The whole area was hot from the event. People could not understand what had happened. They just looked at the hill of ashes where the house used to be.

Fleming picked up his radio and said, "Cummings, have some of your people go and check the house to see if there is anything left underground. Do not take any chances, and keep your suits on. And send away the curious people; tell them that some lightning hit a gas reservoir."

Cummings said, "Good idea, but I still don't understand what happened here. You guys should leave, and we will meet at the base."

Fleming said, "Roger, see you there in an hour."

The two US command cars left as fire trucks rushed to the scene, their sirens breaking the silence of the night. The Canadian agents, in their chemical suits, rushed people back to their homes.

Simon looked exhausted. Sarah asked, "My love, are you all right?"

Simon said, "I want water to drink. My mouth is dry." Walker gave him a small water bottle. Simon quickly gulped it down and requested another one. He was really thirsty.

They arrived at the military base, and the military police at the gate let them in, as they'd been ordered to previously. Once in the conference room, the teams took their suits off, and one of the agents took a Geiger counter and checked everyone for radiation. No one was contaminated. Once they all were done, they sat around the table. All had burning questions on their lips. They almost all asked at the same time, "What was that? And who fired it?"

Fleming said, "This will be on a need-to-know basis. No one can discuss what transpired here tonight, not even to your families. This is branded top secret." He picked up his mobile phone and called the boss of the CIA, Tanner.

Fleming said, "Hi. Operation Fire has been 100 per cent successful. We will be leaving soon. We are waiting for the Canadian forces to come back, and we still have to give some kind of explanation. I don't know what to say."

Tanner said, "You don't know – that's the answer. Maybe something exploded from inside the house. That is the only explanation for the moment. I will inform the president. Let's meet at my office in Washington when you arrive. We have a lot to discuss."

Fleming said, "OK, bye." He looked at Simon with curiosity and thought, *He is a secret weapon in himself.* Simon had fallen asleep in his mother's lap. Simon was just a five-year-old child, but Fleming saw the power of this child with an angelic face.

Forty-five minutes later, the Canadian commandos arrived. They took their suits off, refreshed, and came to join the Americans at the conference table.

Cummings looked as if he had been betrayed. He cleared his throat and said, "What was all this about? No one fired, and it looked like a nuclear explosion. Can you explain?"

Fleming said, "We were there like you. We did not fire, and there was no other weapon. If you didn't shoot, maybe they had a bomb inside that they detonated by accident? Did your guys check for radiation and if the terrorists had an escape route?"

"No, all six were dead, just badly burned bones," Cummings said. "The entire yard has disappeared, leaving a ten-foot-deep giant crater in that property. It ends exactly at the legal border, and there's no damage to any of the neighbours' grass or property. This is very, very strange. I don't see any reasonable explanation."

"I agree, even now that I have all the facts," Fleming said.

"We left all the property sealed off. In the morning, our scientific crews will have to find an explanation for all this."

"If you don't mind, I will send an FBI team to assist you guys. Now we have to leave; I have to report on tonight's actions."

"Your plane has been refuelled and is ready to go," Cummings said.

All stood up. Sarah picked up Simon in her arms. He was a bit heavy. Agent Walker understood and offered to carry him, and Sarah accepted gladly.

Both crews shook hands with their counterparts and exited the conference room. Fleming thanked Cummings, and a small bus picked up all the Americans and dropped them by their plane.

The pilots were ready, and the engines were already running. Sarah went up first, followed by Walker carrying Simon in his arms. Then Fleming and the rest of the crew boarded. The plane taxied and then took off.

Sarah was looking at Simon, who was asleep in the seat next to her. She was worried. Simon hadn't budged since being placed in the seat. He was still a bit wet from the sweat, and the moisture was now cold. She touched his forehead. He seemed OK, but she was still worried.

Sarah said, "Agent Walker, I am concerned about Simon."

Agent Walker said, "He's probably just tired, but if you want, we do have a doctor on board."

"Yes, please," Sarah said. "It's not like him to sleep with all this noise around."

Walker left and came back with a man that she hadn't seen or paid attention to until now. He approached and said, "Hi, I am Dr Gold. If you allow me, I will check him out."

The doctor checked Simon's pulse. It was a little high, and Simon was sweaty. After a few moments he said, "The boy seems to be exhausted. Has he exerted himself greatly?"

Sarah said, "Yes, he has. I cannot state what at this moment, but yes, he did."

The doctor, "Whatever it was must have been very stressful and intense. Let him sleep it off. He will be OK."

Fleming said, "That's good. We still have an hour and thirty minutes to get to destination; let him sleep. He has done an incredible job. I can hardly believe what I've seen. No one will believe it. Thank G-d I have it recorded on video."

"Yes, you are right," Sarah said with a bit of apprehension. She was still afraid of what all this would lead to. Simon was not even six years old.

Fleming went to the cockpit to make a call. Sarah covered Simon with a thin blanket that the stewardess gave her. Simon was very quiet and breathing slower; he was getting to a normal state.

It was six in the morning when they finally arrived. Simon awakened and asked, "Where are we, Mommy?"

Sarah said, "Hi, darling. We have just arrived. Are you OK?"

Simon said, "Yes, I am just a little sleepy. Are we going home?"

"We are going to the hotel, where everyone is waiting for us. You will rest then. You were courageous there; you did great."

Fleming and Walker approached, and Fleming said, "So, little hero, you are awake. You did great. The virus was totally eliminated, thanks to you."

Walker said, "That was great, big man. Come with me now; I will take you to your hotel."

They all got off the plane, and after they said goodbye to Fleming, Walker took Sarah and Simon in a black Cadillac to their hotel.

The whole family was there and asleep. They had four rooms – one for each set of grandparents, one for the children, and one for Sarah. They were very nice and luxurious rooms. It was morning already, and Sarah had to close the shades. Simon slept in Sarah's room for the night, and they both went to sleep.

The Day Simon Was Discovered

Dan and Jacob woke at eight thirty and checked to see if Sarah and Simon had returned. They pushed Sarah's door that was a bit open Once they saw the two sleeping, they felt good. They still did not know what was really going on. Simon finally woke up around ten o'clock and awakened Sarah. She could barely open her eyes. She noticed Simon smiling at her and smiled back.

She stood and asked, "Are you hungry, my love?"

"Starving," Simon said.

Sarah suggested, "Let's order breakfast in the room."

"Great!"

Sarah ordered room service and then had the hotel front desk connect her to her parents' room. Her mother answered, "Hello?"

"Hi, Mom," Sarah said. "We are here in the room. We ordered breakfast. Can you all come?"

Her mother said "Of course. I'll tell the others. See you soon."

There was a knock at the door, and Simon opened. It was the room service. Sarah and Simon looked at the food as if they were seeing food for the first time. After tipping the steward, they jumped on the food.

Ten minutes later there was another knock at the door. Simon, holding a cup of hot cocoa, answered the door. It was the whole family. Lilly ran to Simon and hugged him and then to Sarah. They all kissed each other, and then Jacob asked, "So, what happened? And why are we all here in Washington?"

Sarah said, "Well, this of course is top secret. They specifically dictated what we could tell you." She told them almost everything, omitting just a few details of the operation.

They all hung on to every word. If a person had overheard them, he or she would think that they were talking about a science fiction movie.

Once Sarah was done, Dan asked, "What now? How long are we staying here in Washington?"

Sarah said, "I do not know yet, but I am sure that we will find out soon enough."

Eric was quiet and was holding Simon by the shoulder. By his eyes, it was clear that his little brother had impressed him.

The phone rang. Dan was the closest and picked it up. "Hello?"

"Good morning, this is Agent Walker. Could I speak to Mrs Sarah Hirsh please?"

Dan said, "Good morning, Agent Walker, this is Dan, Sarah's father. How are you?"

"Great, thank you. Is everyone OK?"

"Yes, we are still in the dark but healthy. Let me get Sarah. Here she is. Bye for now."

"Good morning, Agent Walker," Sarah said.

"Good morning, Mrs Hirsh. I hope that you and Simon are rested! We have a prepared programme for Simon today."

"What kind of programme?"

"I will tell you in person, when we meet."

"At what time?"

Agent Walker said, "It is ten thirty now. How about noon? The scheduled programme starts at one o'clock."

"I guess that it is OK."

"Great, see you then!" Agent Walker said and hung up.

Everyone was looking at Sarah with questioning expressions. Finally she said, "The FBI has scheduled something for Simon today. I don't know what yet. They are coming to pick us up at noon."

Jacob said, "But you guys must be tired. They have to let you rest."

David's mother said, "I don't think that Sarah and Simon have a say in this decision."

Sarah said, "Well, we will go and see where all this is leading us."

Dan said, "I think that the government is building too much on Simon. They have to realise that even though he has a certain power, he also is a small child. He must act and play like a regular kid. He needs space to be a child and to be in playgrounds and school."

"I agree with you, Dad," Sarah said. "Let's see what today brings. Let's not speculate for now. I promise I will ask the pertinent questions today." She just wanted to reassure her dad.

They all left the room to let Sarah and Simon get ready. Simon had to go to the children's room to get new fresh clothes.

At noon there was a knock at the door of Sarah's room, and Sarah opened the door. It was Agent Walker. "Hi, Mrs Hirsh. Are you ready?"

Sarah said, "Yes, I am. I just have to pick Simon up from the children's room." She closed the door behind her and knocked at the next one, just beside her room.

Lilly opened the door. "Hi, Mommy. You are all dressed, can I go with you guys "?
"Only Simon and I are going," Sarah said. "You will spend the day with Eric and your grandparents. You will have a good time, my darling."

"But, Mommy, I want to spend some time with you and Dad – I mean, Simon."

"I promise, baby, that we will be together very soon. Come, Simon; they are waiting for us."

Simon was dressed in grey slacks, a white shirt, and a blue blazer. He really looked like a little man.

Agent Walker said, "Hi, Simon. How are you this morning?"

"Good, thank you, Agent Walker," Simon replied.

Agent Walker said, "Good to hear. Today is an important day."

The three left and took the black Cadillac that they had used the night before.

Once in the car, Sarah asked, "Agent Walker, can I know where are we are going and for what?"

"We are going to the Library of Congress, here in Washington. It's been closed to the public and reserved for a conference between Simon and the greatest minds of our country, maybe of the world. There will be scientists from every field – medicine, nuclear physics, mathematics, religion, and much more. They will test Simon's knowledge and powers. It's a great honour for Simon. They all came from all over the country."

Sarah asked, "What will they do to him?"

"Just ask questions, from the simplest to the most-complicated ones, to evaluate the degree of his genius. No one will touch him; this I promise."

Sarah said, "This is interesting. I would like to know more about my son as well."

Agent Walker said, "As I told you, it's a great honour. This is the first time ever that it has been done. Mr Fleming and Mr Tanner of the CIA organised it. Simon is an incredibly valuable national asset. I have seen first-hand what he can do, and it's beyond words. We're having some problems with the Canadian secret service because they still cannot comprehend what happened over there. There is no weapon that could do that. They keep bugging Mr Fleming to tell them what happened."

Sarah asked, "So what you guys are going to do?"

"We will continue denying and let them continue wondering and forming hypotheses about what happened."

Sarah kept quiet for a few moments. She seemed to be lost in her thoughts. Walker interrupted her thoughts, announcing, "We have arrived."

It was a beautiful giant building. They got out of the car. At the entrance of the building was a big sign that read, "The Library of Congress will be closed until tomorrow for maintenance." They entered the Great Hall. Three security officers and two men in dark suits, probably FBI agents, stood behind a very large desk at the centre with metal detectors. Agent Walker presented his badge, and the two men in dark suits said to the security officers, "They are OK; let them in." The security officers handed them three passes and let them through.

Agent Walker asked one of the agents, "Is everyone here, or are we the first?"

The agent said, "Everyone is here; you are the last. Even the bosses are here."

They went through a hallway; they could overhear conversations coming from behind one of the walls in front of them. The more they walked, the louder the voices became. They arrived to a double door; a plaque stated that it was a projection room. They opened the doors to reveal a movie theatre layout. The room was crowded with people, and everyone turned to look at the newcomers.

There was silence for a moment. All those present concentrated their attention on the little boy. They probably already had information on Simon. On the lower level of the theatre at the centre, Fleming and Tanner smiled and opened their arms in a sign of welcome when they saw Simon.

Fleming said, "Hi, Simon. Please come over here."

Walker and Sarah took two available seats in the third row, and Simon went straight down to join the two bosses without any shyness or confusion. He looked natural and at ease. He shook hands with Fleming and Tanner and turned to face the public. There were about 130 people – scientists, professors, engineers, doctors, physicists, and so on.

Fleming said, "Ladies and gentlemen, doctors, professors, and men of science, I have the pleasure and the privilege to present to you Simon Hirsh." There was a loud and warm applause. "Can you say a few words, Simon?"

Simon in a natural way took the microphone from Fleming. Sarah was so proud to see Simon acting like a grown-up, not embarrassed or shy, as a five-year-old would be.

Simon said, "Hi, everyone. My name is Simon David Hirsh." Sarah was shocked at him using David, his father's name. He continued, "I am five years old and was born in Chicago, Illinois.

I lost my father before I was born; he was murdered. I have a brother, Eric, and a sister, Lilly. My mother is Sarah, sitting there." He pointed to her. "I understand that you all want to ask me questions. I have not prepared for your questions, as I do not know what the questions will be."

Tanner said, "Dear Simon, the present will ask questions without stating or identifying themselves, in order to avoid confusing you and to make this conference shorter." Simon nodded in approval, and to the public Tanner said, "Please stand up when you speak. The list in front of you gives the order of who will speak when. Thank you."

Fleming asked, "Will the first speaker please stand?"

A man in his fifties stood up and said, "Hi, Simon. I read that you were born dead and that you were revived. What can you tell us about that? What do you remember?"

Simon said, "Well, I remember everything, beginning with my father's thoughts, or let us say mine. I remember the day I was murdered and all the happenings since then. My soul incorporated into my dead son's body. I remember my stay in heaven for so many months. The moment they found out that the baby had no soul, I was projected like a laser beam into my own son's lifeless body."

Another person stood up and asked, "What is heaven, or paradise, like?"

Simon said, "Paradise is the optimum of a soul's trek. The purpose of our various reincarnations is to complete the cycle of cleansing our souls, understanding that the soul is positive energy in this material world and in paradise. The final destination is to incorporate into the endless light of the Creator, G-d Almighty. Not so in hell, where the soul turns to negative energy. We will probably discuss that later.

"I do remember leaving this world through a tunnel of light, but before that, during the first seven days of my demise, I hovered between worlds. I could see and hear everything going on at my house and in the cemetery. I could see, hear, and feel my family's pain and sorrow. To my surprise, my daughter, Lilly, could see and talk to me. Poor darling, everyone thought that she was suffering a nervous breakdown.

"And at the cemetery, I met many souls that were waiting for the beings of light, what we call angels, that marked a soul's departure towards the tunnel of light. The beings of light normally came seven days after death, as they did with me, to explain to the deceased how to proceed once in the tunnel of light. My mind was opened to them. My entire life played like a movie. There was nothing that I could hide from these beings. At that moment you are an open book. Their instructions were to go down the tunnel until the light that came from the end – the endless light – became unbearable. Then I was to take the first gate to my right, and that is what I did."

The assembly applauded, and a man in the first row stood up and asked, "What was inside that gate?"

Simon said, "It was paradise at my level of purity. It was so peaceful. I joined many other souls that were at the same level of purity as me, and we were all in a way somewhat connected. There was no hunger, pain, sorrow, or worries. It was simply fantastic. The only thing we all wanted was to be present for the special events when heaven opened. At those times we saw above us the special master beings of light, or archangels, and many other kinds of light beings. And at the end we glimpsed the endless light. We had forgotten about our passages on earth, and our only wish was to reach higher realms, to upgrade our energy to be to able reach the Creator. That is not possible in paradise and can only be accomplished by reincarnating in the material world."

Sarah was totally dumbfounded; the voice was David's, but it was coming from Simon's little mouth. The whole assembly could not utter a word. The answers came out so naturally. It was so quiet the assembled people's breathing could be heard.

A lady stood up and asked, "How many gates or levels of paradise are there? And where is paradise?"

Simon said, "Paradise is four dimensional, just like this world. Paradise's four dimensions are subdivided into ten levels, and each of those ten levels is again subdivided into ten more, endlessly. So when a person is born, he or she has a certain level or degree of purity of positive energy. When that person passes away from our material world, his or her level of purity determines what level of paradise that soul goes to.

"Of course, there is a minimum of positive energy a departing soul must reach to reincarnate as a human being. Souls can be reincarnated into four different types of being: humans, animals, plants, and the inanimate, like stone, dust, minerals, and any other earthly material. And just as the four different dimensions are subdivided, each type has many levels.

"As to where heaven is, if the universe was in the form of a human body, paradise would be the brain."

Again there was a vast round of applause. Cameras were filming the whole conference.

An older gentleman with white hair stood up. "Hi. Do you know how large the universe is?"

Simon said, "To understand the magnitude of the universe, let's continue to use the human body as a metaphor. If the universe is a human body, our galaxy, the Milky Way, is a single atom in the body. Our sun is a proton; and the planets are the neutrons and all the particles within the atom. The electrons or leptons would be the stars, which act as gluons and keep our galaxy together. So it won't be too complicated to calculate the real size of the Universe..."

There was another big round of applause, and everyone got to their feet.

A woman stood up and asked, "Keeping on the same subject, what surrounds the universe? And what are black holes?"

Simon said, "What surrounds the universe is the endless light, or the Creator's essence – pure intelligence energy. His essence is everywhere. Nothing comes to being without his essence. A new galaxy cannot be formed without that energy. It would be like a baby that was born dead, like myself. They both need a derivation of the Creator's essence; the baby needs a soul, and the galaxy needs the energy. In a way, a baby being born is the same as a galaxy coming into existence.

"For you all to understand black holes, I will keep using the body as a simple comparison. It suffices to explore the human body to better understand our complex universe. Black holes are the digestive apparatus of the universe. Anything that goes through does not disappear but just goes to a different dimension, just as our stomachs convert food into positive or negative energies that are transferred to our blood and then to the needed parts of our bodies."

Fleming stood up and said, "Ladies and gentlemen, let's take a break and have lunch. I am sure that everyone is hungry, especially Simon. We will meet back here in one hour."

Sarah, Simon, Fleming, Walker, and Tanner went together to have a late lunch in a nearby restaurant.

Tanner said, "Simon, not many people can impress me, but you sure have. This is the first time ever that anyone has come back to life and told us everything that the world has ever wanted to know about what happens after death."

Fleming said, "I join my colleague in his statement. You left all the greatest minds speechless. You are our greatest asset ever."

All these compliments did not mean anything to Simon, but they made Sarah proud.

They finished lunch and went back to the conference. Some of the scientists had not left, instead forming a few small groups, probably by related professions, to have heated discussions about what they had heard from this phenomenon child.

No one paid attention to Simon and the bosses until Tanner said, "Ladies and gentlemen, we will start in five minutes. Please take your seats."

Everyone did. Silence gradually filled the conference room. A new round of applause started, and all stood on their feet again to greet Simon for the second part of the conference.

Simon said, "I see that you now have more questions than before. I would like to convey to all of you that I gave you answers in a simplistic way not as a sign of disrespect but so that we will have enough time to answer all your questions. I am sure that we will see each other again, and then we will be able to discuss each matter in more detail. Thank you."

Fleming said, "Let us resume the questions."

A blond man in his forties who was built like a wrestler stood up and said, "You have spoken about heaven, but what about hell? What is it like, and where is it?"

Simon looked at the man with a grim expression. He lowered his gaze and said, "Oh, hell, it is and always will be the main source of our problems. Greed, lust, and selfishness allow hell to exist. Hell is an earthly location only.

"When we are born, our souls come with a certain degree of purity. For the sake of an explanation, let's that a new soul has a positive value of 1,250 and that you gain or lose points throughout each reincarnation. To reincarnate as a human, your soul needs at least 1,000 points. To reincarnate as an animal, you need 500 points, and to reincarnate as a plant, you just need any positive points. If you have negative points, you reincarnate as a mineral. This is the only level that has no way of returning, since it is the one type of negative energy.

"For this person the body is everything, so this person will stay with his or her body until the ground absorbs all of his or her essence. As we know, fuel comes from fossils, from bodies. It takes thousands of years, but this person's body eventually becomes fuel. The person's essence flows slowly towards the magma, or hell, at the centre of the earth. As we say, this person burns in hell. You have to understand that the negative energy that was this individual has full awareness of the actual situation. The time it takes for this to happen does not reflect earthly time, since time and distance are human inventions."

All those present in the conference room listened, and most took notes. None were able to comment. Everything they knew and had learned was obsolete. This had them completely confused. The applause wasn't energetic this time. This answer was a hard pill to swallow. It made them doubt what they had believed all these years, and it destroyed the foundational belief that after death there was nothing. When Simon had spoken earlier about heaven, they had not made too much of it, and they had not had time to think or speak about it.

Fleming said, "Next one please."

A young, nice-looking woman stood up. "Hi. What climatic dangers and changes can we expect to face within the coming decades? Is the damage reversible?"

Simon said, "Well, the climatic changes that the earth is going through are really bad for various reasons. First, deserts are overtaking green land. As humans need to rest every seventh day, the earth needs to rest every seventh year to be able to re-energise. If you recharge a battery nonstop, after some time the

143

battery will stop holding a charge. For example, Africa used to be the greenest land anywhere, but today a very large part has become desert, and water is difficult to find. It is possible to reverse these climatic changes by following certain principles and actions.

"Negative is winning over positive. This is a very serious situation. If the world's community does not make a 180-degree U-turn, civilisation as we know it today will end. We will go back to the Stone Age, and after that the human race will disappear within 1,000 years. At the pace we are going, we will auto-destruct within 50 to 100 years.

"When I speak of negativity, I mean that the humans will cause a nuclear war that will create a domino effect. A very small part of the world population will be the cause of this nuclear holocaust. The world is closing an eye. People do not think that this will affect them personally. Instead of looking for alternative energy sources that serve the future of the world, they instead serve the destroyer or the negative influence. They use fossil fuels as the ultimate blackmail tool against energy-dependent Third World countries.

"This fuel in itself is also a destroyer in another spectrum. As you all now know, that fuel is the most negative energy. It comes from hell and is the black energy of souls with very bad intelligence energy. This energy is released constantly and is poisoning our atmosphere and the ozone layer. Even though fossil fuels have helped evolution, we have now become addicted to that energy over the decades we spent without finding alternative energies. Now fossil fuels are a drug to the world's economy. Now this infernal poison and our dependency on it are ruling the world. Hell is ruling the world.

"Of course, let's not go into religious euphoria. Let me simplify this and take it out of scientific terms for the sake of time. In addition to the air contamination, all these nonstop energy releases mean we also will stop feeding the earth's magma. This will cause the earth to dry, and in a few decades, the magma will cool off and slowly die. This will affect the earth's gravity, and the earth will shift out of place in the galaxy. Once this happens, life will be non-existent. Of course this is the worst-case scenario.

"All this negative power comes from a few people who slowly are controlling our destiny and the world's very shaky future. Not only that, they are using this negative power against good people, and they have bought the free world's conscience with this energy.

"Today, the world blames everything on the victims and defends the world's terrorists. Look at the United Nations. They exist for the sole purpose of blaming and condemning the victims. Dictators have control of more than 50 per cent of that black gold. In the next five years, earthquakes, tsunamis, and hurricanes will be part of our daily lives. The weather will change polarities. The cold countries will become hot, and the hot ones will freeze. That is what we all have to expect. So I would say that we face a very bad future in many, many ways. Sorry, but this is not just a prediction but also a fact."

All the faces in the conference looked pale and very disappointed. These men and women had come full of curiosity and thirsty for knowledge, but they'd just heard doomsday predictions – no future for their children and families. Even Fleming, Tanner, and Walker seemed disgusted and had signs of deep sadness written all over their faces.

The next person who stood up was a young scientist. "The question I have has nothing to do with my specialty, but how sure are you of your statements? Is there a solution to stop the process of all that you have said?"

Simon said, "All that I have said will happen with 100 per cent certainty if the world continues under the same regime. But the answer to your second question is *yes*, definitely. What has to be done? Beginning tomorrow, not next week, the United States should help lead the world in enacting the following changes.

145

"First, oil pumping has to be reduced 20 per cent per year. Oil drilling should be completely stopped in five years maximum. If countries will not comply, their oil reservoirs should be destroyed, and the black market should not exist in any way possible.

"Second, the world science community should work on new non-polluting energies as if the world was coming to an end in a week. Do not forget that it is your children's and families' futures that you are fighting for. Although solar energy is a bit more expensive right now, once everyone starts buying this equipment, costs will reduce by 80 per cent. For now, the costs will be the least of your worries.

"Third, let the earth rest. Stop burying nuclear waste, and find real solutions to get rid of it. This also should begin immediately, and nuclear waste should be reduced 30 per cent per year. I will help the different types of researchers in any way I can.

"Fourth, we will need to entertain a full-scale war and destroy terrorism to the core, as if terrorism was the most virulent cancer or virus. This should be done without mercy. Any country that will not work to eradicate terrorists should be considered as much a terrorist as the others. By sheltering terrorists, these countries allow terrorism to survive. This can no longer be acceptable under any circumstances. Do not think that this is too dramatic. Time is very short. If within a decade or two you haven't succeeded, then the end of life will begin.

"Fifth, the world has to regain its consciousness and pride. It cannot be otherwise. All the world's populations have to give a hand in this gigantic task. World citizens will have to compromise to help their respective governments, spending at least two hours a day in national duty. If we want to survive, every human from fifteen years and older will have to help, even if it's just something small, like taking garbage from the streets or separating recycling from garbage.

"Sixth, countries that have high birth rates should implement birth control measures, limiting to two children per family. More than that, families with more than two children should be penalised. These measures would reduce poverty and famine. Overpopulation indirectly increases human migration to many countries. With high numbers of migrants, more people are unemployed, and employers take advantage of poor migrants. All this generates hate, crime, and much more. Poor countries' citizens cannot expect to have sex, make children, and force other people pay for them. This is total selfishness. Nothing should be too much to buy a future for our children and our children's offspring.

"Ladies and gentlemen, I did not come here to scare you but to tell you the truth. The time is now. I assure all of you that I have not exaggerated what I've told you today. I will sit down and argue with any of you and prove this to you in scientific terms. Please do not waste even one hour, because that particular hour will never come back. The negative forces are moving very fast. They are a virus, and we are and should be the antibodies. If they grow too fast, they can overcome the antibodies. Then the cancer will become generalised, and death will be pronounced. Do not allow this.

"I feel that some of you are sceptic about everything I have just said. I wish that I was wrong. I know that you are all scientists; I do have a way to prove everything I've said. I ask that anyone who suffers from high blood pressure or a heart condition to leave. I will take the rest to the year 2020, and you will see for yourselves what will happen if we do not make a move immediately. It will be very shocking. So no one will say that what is about to happen is hypnosis, each one of you can take one inanimate object from that future, and you will still have that item back in our actual time."

They all looked at each other and spoke between them. It was incredible. This little child was going to take them into the future;

147

they were going to travel in time. Even though they were sceptic, they were excited about the thought.

An older man stood up and said, "I have a question about this time travel and about older people like me who could die any day or anytime. Let's say I'm supposed to die by 2011. If I go to 2020, where I'm supposed to be dead, what will happen then?"

Simon said, "I understand your concern. But you will only be travelling to the year 2020, not living in that year. If you should be dead by then, you will simply not see yourself there. You will just be a time traveller. We will spend one whole day in the future, but the trip will last only an hour of our time. So, to answer your question, you have nothing to worry about to that end. Each of you should bring one very small container that can be tightly sealed to take a sample of your interest. Also bring a plastic Ziploc bag to put the container in. You can also bring a small camcorder with a full battery charge."

Fleming said, "I think that we will leave this travel into the future for tomorrow morning so that you will all have time to prepare. It's getting late, so let's take one more question for today. Whoever is next, please ask your question."

A pretty young blonde woman, very elegant, stood up and asked, "Since you were in paradise and know so much about everything, which is the true religion? And what would you suggest to the ones who uphold the other religious beliefs?"

Simon said, "I'm surprised that no one asked that question sooner. My answer will probably surprise you. In a way religions are a map into the future with various shepherds, or guides if you prefer. The guides have a certain divine knowledge; I am not pointing at a certain religion.

"Life for every individual has a beginning, birth, and an end, death. It is called the life of the line. Religious guides and teachings are supposed to guide you through life. So religions have dos and don'ts, and following those precepts is supposed to make your trek safer. In a way religion is a map guiding you through a jungle.

"The roads are many, but many are full of traps. So the guidance of your religion should bring you to safe port, even though the road may be longer and full of temptations and traps. The dos and don'ts create for you a shield. Your way of getting to the end will buy you more points to go through the tunnel of light.

"I know that you want me to tell you which religion is the good one. It is simpler than you all might think. You should see if your religion demands that you do cruel things or kill in its name. These are the no-nos of where I come from. They will send you directly to the other end of the spectrum, down below.

"The simplest rule is to love thy neighbour as thyself. In other words, don't do to others what you do not want others to do to you. That should be the way of the heart. Trust your heart to find the guidance or the true religion to help you get to the other side as safely as possible. Of course you should do as much as you can to help others without forcing your beliefs or religion upon them. Just be a Good Samaritan, and you will get more points, or positive energy, to reach the highest gate in the world of the endless light."

Fleming said, "Ladies and gentlemen, let's wrap it up for today; it's already late. We will meet tomorrow morning at nine o'clock."

There was a big round of applause, and all began to leave. One man in his fifties came down towards Fleming, Simon, and Tanner and shook hands with Tanner and Fleming.

Fleming said, "Hello, Dr Stern. Here, meet Simon."

Dr Stern said, "The conference was great; I would say incredible. It was very inspiring. It is a pleasure to meet you, Simon, if I may call you so." He extended his hand, and Simon shook it warmly.

Fleming said, "Simon, Dr Stern is the president's personal physician."

Simon nodded and smiled but with a very strange look on his face. "Glad to meet you," he said. His mood had changed, as if meeting the doctor bothered him. The change did not go unnoticed by Fleming and Tanner. The doctor said goodbye and left.

Tanner asked, "Is something wrong?" Fleming asked the same question in echo.

Simon asked, "Can we go somewhere else to talk? Mom, can you sit here and wait? We won't be long."

Sarah said, "Yes, darling, I will."

Fleming said, "Yes, of course, let's go to another room."

The three went to a small office at the end of the hallway. Shelves filled with books covered three of the walls of the room. Once inside Fleming and Tanner sat and looked at Simon anxiously to see what had bothered him when he'd met the doctor.

Fleming asked, "What is it, Simon?"

Simon asked, "Are you still looking for Rasputin?"

Both men froze, staring at Simon. Rasputin was the master Russian spy. No one knew who he was or what he looked like. The CIA had given him the code name Rasputin, and only a handful of people knew about him.

Tanner asked, "What do you know about him? And what does this have to do with the president's physician?"

Simon said, "Forty-five years ago, an American couple gave birth to identical twins in New York. One of the babies was taken from the nursery and was never found."

Fleming and Tanner listened attentively, wondering where this was leading.

Simon continued, "Well, this child, as you've probably guessed, was taken by the KGB and raised in a special house in Russia. They spoke to him only in English so that he wouldn't have a Russian accent that would be hard to hide. After he turned twenty, he learned Russian language and studied political science."

The two men were fascinated and waited in suspense to finally find out who Rasputin was.

Simon continued, "At the age of twenty-three, the twin brother was kidnapped from the University of Oxford. The Russian-raised twin took his place and had information about every single detail of his life. So it was easy to replace him. No one has noticed; even his girlfriend, Nancy, did not see the difference."

Tanner jumped out of his chair. "My G-d, is it Barry O'Malley, our president? That is impossible."

Fleming said, "Simon, do you know what you are implying? This cannot be." The information fell like an atomic bomb.

Tanner asked, "How sure are you?"

Simon said, "I'm 100 per cent sure. When I touched the doctor's hand, I saw everything clearly. No doubt about it."

Tanner asked, "What if we organised a personal interview with the president?"

Simon said, "You can be sure that he will refuse, especially if he knows everything about me. If I can, I will find out who else in this administration might be involved."

"Let's try it," Fleming said. "My G-d, this could bring down the US. He's been in the White house for six months already. He already knows a lot about everything, and he does know about Simon."

Tanner said, "He – or, I should say, they – have fooled all of us. How could we have suspected a real all-American family? We checked him from A to Z when he became involved in politics and rechecked him again when he became senator of New York."

Fleming said, "If not for Simon, no one would have ever doubted him. Who would imagine that the head honcho of our country was the master Russian spy who we've been looking for, for twenty years? We'd begun to believe that he was just a myth."

Tanner said, "After thinking about all this, Simon is right. We will see what he says about meeting Simon. If he refuses or gives any kind of excuse, then we will know for sure. How will we proceed after that? We have no proof, and everyone will think that we are both crazy."

"Let's wait until we finish the conference tomorrow, and then we will talk about it," Fleming said. "Maybe Simon will help us and tell us how to proceed without becoming the world's laughing stock for having a Russian President."

Simon said, "You have just one solution, and it is to kill him. You cannot prove anything, and up to now, he hasn't made a false move. He will be activated as a spy only for a very tough mission that could be fatal and a checkmate for the US."

Fleming said, "Let's go now; your mother is waiting. We will take you to your hotel."

Tanner said to Fleming, "We have to put a full security team in place. Now, Simon will become a major target."

Fleming said, "They'll have guards around the clock. I will organise four teams of four agents. They'll take shifts of eight hours, so each team will overlap two hours with the next team."

Tanner said, "OK, let's go for now. I will put some of my teams in the buildings around the hotel, and we will have electronic surveillance as well."

Sarah was waiting in the conference room looking sleepy. When they arrived, she stood up and smiled. Seeing their faces, she knew that something was very wrong. She was an intelligent and intuitive woman. She did not ask; she knew that if they wanted to tell her, they would.

They spoke for five minutes and then left for the hotel. Fleming ordered Agent Walker, who had waited with Sarah in the conference room, to organise the protection teams and to supervise them. Agent Walker was to stay at the hotel and take a room next to Simon's. Agent Walker also had a feeling that something was very wrong.

Once in the hotel, Sarah and Simon went to their rooms, where the whole family was waiting. Sarah gave more or less a recount of what had transpired in the course of the day. They went to bed after a very long and tiring day.

Sarah could not sleep that night. She felt that something was going really wrong; it might be her mother's instinct. All these agents were guarding them day and night, and secrets were being kept from her even though she was Simon's mother. Tanner and Fleming had started conversing with Simon as if he were the commander in chief. This situation was so weird, and if Tanner and Fleming feared for the family, it meant that something must be really wrong.

Simon slept soundly. Sarah looked at him tenderly, proud of who he was – her son and, in a way, David. He reminded her so much of the husband she'd lost. At that time she'd thought that it was the end of the world for her. G-d had seen her suffering and taken pity on her by sending this wonderful child. Since he'd been born, not one day had been boring, though some days had been scary.

Time-Travelling into the Future

The night seemed endless for Sarah. She probably looked at her watch a hundred times. At six o'clock she got up and took a shower to refresh and then made a strong coffee to stay awake. She let Simon sleep for another hour.

She went to go see Eric and Lilly in their room. When they had arrived the previous night, the kids had been asleep already. Once in the hallway, Sarah noticed four agents, two at each end of the hallway. So as she thought, things were really serious. They all nodded good morning as Sarah went to the next room, where the children were.

Inside, it was still dark; the shades were closed. Lilly was sleeping soundly. She looked like a little angel with her tiny nose. She'd loved her father beyond comprehension, and after his passing she'd transferred that love to her younger brother. Eric was already a big boy, and he had so many of David's traits and gestures, even David's way of speaking.

Eric had heard his mother open the door and asked, "Is that you, Mom?"

Sarah said, "Yes, darling. When I came back last night, you were asleep, and I did not want to wake you up." She sat down next to him, kissed his hand, and explained more or less about the previous day, without entering into details. Lilly woke up and came to Eric's bed. She kissed her mom and sat on her lap. She wanted to be pampered, and she was.

Now it was about seven o'clock, and it was time to go and awaken Simon. Sarah told the kids to get ready. She then woke her parents and asked them to take care of the kids because she and Simon had another long day ahead of them.

Her mother said, "Don't worry; go and do what you have to do. The kids will be OK."

Sarah went to her room and found Simon still asleep. Yesterday had been an exhausting day for him. He'd made a lot of efforts to connect himself to all the knowledge in the higher spheres, and that probably was really hard for a five-year-old child or, for that matter, anyone.

She caressed his face and kissed him. "Hi, baby! It's time to wake up! It's seven thirty. Wake up!"

Simon stretched out and said, "Hi, Mom. It's already morning? I am so tired!"

"I know, darling, and you are going to have another long and tiring day. Go take a shower and get ready. I will prepare your clothes for you. Go."

Against his will, he stood up and went to the shower. Sarah prepared everything for him and ordered breakfast to the room.

Twenty minutes later, there was a knock at the door, and a voice said from behind the door, "Room service."

Before Sarah could open the door, there was a second knock and another voice. "Mrs Hirsh, it's Agent Walker. Can you open the door?"

Sarah opened the door and said, "Good morning, Mr Walker."

"Good morning," Agent Walker replied. "How are you?"

"Good, thank you. Simon will be ready in a minute. We will have breakfast, and then we will leave."

"No, no rush," Agent Walker said. "We just have to check anything coming into your room or your family's rooms. I will be outside waiting."

Sarah asked, "Would you like a coffee?"

"No thanks; I already had some earlier. I will see you soon," Agent Walker said and left the room.

Simon came out dressed, and they sat to have breakfast. Fifteen minutes later, they were ready to leave.

The moment they opened the door, Walker and three other agents were there ready to escort them.

Sarah said, "I will just say bye to my family, and I will follow you. Come, Simon."

They went and said goodbye to the kids and grandparents and then left with the agents. Four other agents were watching the other three rooms where the rest of the family were.

Agent Walker said, "Well, I am curious to see today's experience."

"Will you be joining them?" Sarah asked.

"I would love to, but I think that my boss will want me to supervise security. It's still hard for me to believe that they will physically travel to the future. It sounds unreal."

They arrived to the Library of Congress around nine o'clock. High security could be seen all around the building. The small sign stating that the Library of Congress would be closed for the day was still there.

Sarah and Simon followed Agent Walker inside, and the three other agents closed off the steps behind them. There were agents on the rooftops of the buildings across from the Library of Congress. All this security was not just for Simon but also for all the top scientists in America.

Fleming and Tanner were at the lobby entrance waiting for them. They looked as if they have not slept, and a great worry was written all over their faces. They seemed to have aged overnight.

Fleming said, "Good morning, Mrs Hirsh, and to you too, Simon. Are there are any more instructions as to the travel?"

Simon said, "The people that want to travel to the future should be alone in the conference room. The ones who do not want to go need to leave. The doors should be locked during the travel, as it is imperative that no one goes in or out while we are travelling."

Fleming said, "That will be done. Let's go in and do what we have to do."

Sarah and Simon entered the conference room, followed by Tanner and Walker. It seemed that everyone was present, and they all seemed anxious or sceptic about what they had come to do.

Addressing himself to the scientists in the auditorium, Fleming said, "Anyone who will not be joining our experience will have to leave now. We will begin in twenty minutes." He gave orders to Agent Walker to secure the auditorium from the outside and to have the people who would not be coming stay in an adjacent room.

Simon said, "My mother should stay here; there is no point for her to come. Only scientists will appreciate the tour."

Sarah tried to object, but Fleming had already approved Simon's decision. No one stood up to leave besides the security team, Agent Walker, and Sarah, who did not seem happy to be leaving Simon by himself with all these people.

After that the doors to the entrance of the auditorium were locked and secured. Fleming said to those present, "Well, bravo to all. I see that you are as curious and anxious as I am. Do all of you have your test tubes? And who has brought a camera?"

Five people lifted their cameras into the air.

Tanner asked Simon if he wanted to add anything. Simon nodded and said, "What I need from all of you is a list of places that you want to visit for your tests and observation before we go anywhere. Second, wherever we go, all of you have to stay within fifty yards of me and not venture off alone, or you might not be able to return.

"We will all go to the points of interest together. Mr Fleming and Mr Tanner will be responsible for your security and will be the ones to give the orders. I will only give you technical explanations. If a place could be dangerous, then we will go to the next destination.

"Especially when we are about to move from one point of interest to another, we will have to be practically touching each other. The best thing is to hold each other's hands, and two of you will need to hold my hands. This is a must.

"Also you cannot have in your lists any places where you might see yourselves or family members. This could cause irreparable damage. So please review your and your colleagues' points of interest. This is exclusively a scientific expedition and not for your personal curiosity but for the good of the future of our planet."

Fleming asked, "Does anyone have any questions?"

A young lady stood up and asked, "What could the dangers be for us?"

Simon said, "If everyone follows the rules I've given, nothing bad will happen. But first, I would like to see the list of sites that all of you want to visit."

All the scientists gathered together and discussed all the interesting points to visit. One of them took notes. They formed six groups according to their professions: nuclear physicists, astronomers, medical professionals, aeronautics specialists, mathematicians, and seismologists. Of course within these groups there were various specialties from each of the professions.

Ten minutes later, one of the scientists handed a list to Fleming. The latter thanked him, read it, and then gave it to Tanner. After reviewing it, Tanner said, "First, they want to check the water reservoirs at two or three different places: Washington, New York, and Los Angeles. They also want to test the ground at those three places as well as along the San Andreas fault. They would also like to visit a seismological centre. Then they want to check the sea levels and air pollution in LA, Florida, and New York. They also want to check the air pollution in the centre of the country, around Oklahoma, and visit a tornado weather centre. Finally they want to see some nuclear power plants and the plants' surrounding cities."

The scientist who had handed over the list said, "We would like to take samples of tree leaves, small pieces of tree bark, and seawater. We understand that we cannot take anything alive, like a small fish, to understand the evolution of the pollution of the oceans."

Simon interjected, "You could cut a small piece off of a fish and take that."

The scientist said, "That's good enough for us."

Fleming asked, "Is that all?"

The scientist said, "If possible, we would like to visit two or three volcanoes. Can we go outside of the United States, like to Iceland?"

Simon said, "Yes, where else?"

The scientist replied, "The Yellowstone super volcano and Mount Vesuvius in Italy."

Tanner asked, "Simon, are you sure that we will have time to do all this?"

Simon said, "Yes, we will. It might be over one hour of our time."

Fleming said, "What will you tell the people that we encounter about where we are coming from and what we are doing there?"

By now everyone had gathered around Simon. He answered, "This is a good question. I forgot to mention that when we are there, we will be moving in a different time zone than the local time in the year 2020. We will see them, but they won't be able to see us. We will be moving twenty-four times faster than they are. And this is why twenty-four hours there will be only one hour of our time."

One of the scientists said, "This is very impressive and exciting. What we do not understand is how you are going to take all of us on a voyage into the future."

Simon said, "Well, we are all together seventy-nine people. What I will be doing is overriding all your surrounding lights, or auras, and diverting all your energies into mine. Then I will do what is necessary to teleport us to 2020."

Simon took the list from them and read it. To everyone but Simon this all seemed unreal. They still had doubts that this was going to work. Fleming called everyone to gather around Simon. They had reached the culmination of all the excitement and doubts. They made a tight circle around Simon. Fleming held Simon's right hand, and Tanner held Simon's left. Simon was the centre, so the others held hands and closed the circle.

Simon said, "Please, you should all close your eyes until I say otherwise. It is very important you do this so you won't hurt them. The light will be very bright, and you will feel a bit faint, but do not worry; that is normal. Your energies will be channelled through me. We will go on three. Close your eyes. One, two, three."

Simon was very concentrated, and suddenly very bright and strong lights surrounded the group and began spinning at a very high speed. Of course there was no one there to see it, but Tanner had left a hidden camera to film every single detail. After a few seconds, the entire group had disappeared.

They reappeared at the water reservoirs of Washington, DC, and Simon said, "You can open your eyes now."

Everyone did, and to their pleasant surprise, the transfer had been successful. They applauded Simon. This was the first time in history that someone had travelled in time. At least, no one else had ever claimed to succeed.

Fleming said, "This is beyond any words. I do not know how to express myself. Now everyone please do what we came here to do; let's not waste time."

Three of the scientists went down to the reservoirs. There were various local people dressed in white shirts, but they seemed frozen in place, like statues. The scientists walked between without touching them. Once down next to the water, they put on gloves, pulled a few test tubes from their backpacks, and filled the tubes with water from the main reservoir. The five who had brought cameras filmed the whole scene.

Fleming and Tanner were amazed that this young child had carried seventy-eight people into the future without any equipment or machines.

Fleming said, "Hey, Tanner, are we all in the same dream?"

Tanner said, "I think so. We are all dreaming."

Simon said, "No, you are not dreaming. We are at the water reservoir of Washington, DC, and the year is 2020. Look at the calendar on the wall. We should leave the amazement for the end, when we get back. We should move faster if we want to be able to do everything from the list."

The scientists came back, and Simon asked everyone to join together as they had in the Library of Congress. Everyone did, and the same process repeated. They visited the reservoirs of New York and then Los Angeles.

Once they had finished with the reservoirs, they gathered around Simon, and he said, "According to your list, we will now go and see the same cities to test the ground. We will begin with Washington, DC. Please hold hands."

Again they disintegrated and reappeared in Washington, near the Capitol this time. The streets were full of immobilised people like before. The team walked in between the people. They noticed many differences from the city they had seen that morning on their way to the Library of Congress. There were many cracks on the paved roads. The areas that were supposed to be green were grey and dry in many parts. The trees were partly dry and had no leaves. The greyish grass grounds were sunken in many parts. The sight was really sad to see, especially to people who had seen the area so different that same morning; they were now just some years later. The difference was shocking and sad.

As they walked down the avenue, some of the group collected samples of dust, sand, grass, leaves, and anything that they could test once they got back to their labs. Others used digital equipment they had brought with them to get information about the air purity and air pollution. The sky looked dark and was mostly covered with dark clouds even though it was summer. It looked more like the skies of London.

The group was shocked by what they were seeing. They could no longer see the decadence of their capital. They walked down to the White House. The roads were closed to traffic, and the barricades suggested the instability of the security. It looked more like a military base. Soldiers practically surrounded the White House, and there were small bunkers with big guns to protect against any aircraft with hostile intentions.

Fleming said, "Oh my G-d. It's difficult to speak, and it hurts to swallow. This is a sorrowful sight, and all this is only a few years away. Simon was right and wasn't exaggerating a bit, on the contrary."

Tanner said, "Fleming, you know how many times I've fought this present administration to let us do what we have to do to secure this country from abroad. It is the reason for the CIA's existence. But we are being investigated for anything that they do not like. They want us to take action, but they do not want to know about it."

Simon said, "Gentlemen, what you have seen up to now in nothing. The results of all the tests will be alarming. Let's continue to LA and the San Andreas fault. There you will have the shock of your life."

Fleming called the group to reassemble, which they did immediately, for fear of being left behind in that future.

One of the women asked, "Can we know at least who the president is?"

Simon said, "No, that is not important. We have better things to do. Let's leave now; the task is great."

They joined and teleported very close to the San Andreas fault. When they realised how close they were to the fault, they moved back. They were near the Tejon Pass, and across was the Salton Sea. The sight was grandiose. The geologists took out all kind of digital measuring equipment and began taking notes.

After a few measures one of them exclaimed, "Wow, normally the fault had a steady offset of 2 inches per year. I took notes just before coming, and it has grown 42 inches in the past five years, which means 8.4 inches per year on average. That is over four times greater than the norm. This is really bad, very bad."

They chatted about the possible consequences of this new data.

Another scientist exclaimed, "Is this the beginning of Armageddon?"

Simon said, "Most of you use that term in the wrong manner. The real term in Hebrew is Har Megiddo, or the Mount of Megiddo. It is mentioned in Ezekiel's prophesies that at the end of times, all the forces of Gog and Magog will come to destroy Israel, and the Lord said, 'I will fight those forces and will annihilate them in the plains of Megiddo. And there will be their burial.' So Har Megiddo became Armageddon."

The same person said, "That's good to know; that is the first time that I've heard this explanation. Thank you."

A few scientists were taking dust and gravel samples, and others were filming. They all looked all around and then gathered around Simon.

One asked, "Do you know when this area will sink?"

Simon said, "We will have time to discuss everything once we are back home. Keep notes, and then we will talk about it. Now we should leave; it's time to move."

Every time they had to move, Fleming and Tanner counted the group to be sure that they were not forgetting anyone. It looked weird to see seventy-nine grown-ups converging around a five-year-old child, as if he was their teacher.

They next went to the seismological centre. As usual, the local engineers and workers were immobilised. Just four scientists from the group went to check the seismological records of the past few years. Since the computers were in operation, they did not need passwords to access them. They copied the pertinent data from the computers onto USB drives. The scientists could not believe their eyes. There had been much more land movement and three real earthquakes. Though the earthquakes had not claimed too many lives, they had caused a lot of destruction. California was in real danger. All this land movement and these earthquakes were an omen. They finished all the file copying and rejoined the group.

Now it was time to go to LA, New York, and Florida to verify the coastlines and measure air pollution. They grouped together and departed for these new tasks. It had become almost natural to use this type of transportation.

They showed up on the beach near Marina Del Rey. It was funny to see the waves move in slow motion. The surfers' movements were almost nil, and the swimmers looked weird. On the sand, the people were not moving, at least not what could be noticed.

The group divided itself to the needed tasks. They measured the air pollution and weather. The meteorologist was surprised by the cloudy and grey day; the weather was unusual for that time of the day and of the month.

Another scientist of the group could not believe how the beach had diminished in five years. He had been at this particular beach a week prior to this adventure. He did not have measurements from that particular day, but he was sure that the beach had been wider by at least 30 feet.

They next departed for New York and Florida. The Florida beaches were not as Simon and the others knew; it was really desolating to see. The waterlines were near the hotels, and the sand of these beautiful beaches was under water in various areas. All this had happened in just a few years; they couldn't imagine what it would be like in twenty years. It was unthinkable. Miami, Fort Lauderdale, Palm Beach, and other cities would be completely under water.

Fleming said, "It's a national catastrophe. We have to do a great job when we get back. Please film this; do not miss a single detail."

One of the scientists borrowed a net from a child to catch a small fish. The others took samples of the seawater, algae, air, and sand. The sky started to flash with lightning. A storm was in the making.

Simon said, "We better move. A storm is not good for our time travel. It could distort our point of return. So would you please all gather around me? We have to move now, immediately."

Everyone surrounded Simon, held hands, and disintegrated in a giant cloud of light. As they continued their voyage, time after time the discovery was only really bad news. Everything they saw was in the same line of predictions that Simon had explained and feared.

The twenty-four hours in the future came to term, and they went back to their starting point at the Library of Congress, appearing at the same spot they had left. Everybody smiled to see that they had returned to the auditorium. Everyone looked at his or her watch. Just one hour and five minutes had passed.

Fleming said, "That was quite a trip. We are all exhausted, and it is only eleven fifteen. We have two possibilities. You can all go back to your labs, and we'll meet here tomorrow morning to discuss the answers to all the tests you have taken. Or we can continue the meeting now with any questions you have for Simon. Those in favour of the first option, raise your hands."

Most raised their hands; they had already experienced too many emotions for one day.

Tanner said, "OK, so let's meet here tomorrow morning, let's say ten o'clock."

Everyone stood up. Fleming picked up his walkie-talkie and called Agent Walker to open the doors and come in with Sarah. Once the doors were open, people began leaving. Walker and Sarah came down the stairs towards Simon, Fleming, and Tanner. Simon walked towards his mother, and she hugged him and picked him up in her arms, her heart beating very fast. She said, "Oh, my darling, I was very concerned. Did everything go OK?"

Simon said, "Mom, put me down. You are embarrassing me."

Sarah smiled and put him down. "Sorry, darling, I was just very concerned. So how was your trip?"

Simon said, "Very good and very sad at the same time. Everything that I said was correct. I wish it wasn't. Tomorrow, after they analyse all the samples and data, we will meet to compare the results to today's information."

Fleming said, "Hello, Mrs Hirsh. This was an incredible experience. In my wildest dreams, I could not have imagined that this would be possible one day, let alone in my lifetime. You have to be proud of your son."

Sarah said, "I am, and—"

Tanner interrupted, "I am sorry to interrupt, Mrs Hirsh, but I have to speak urgently with Mr Fleming and Simon. Please, Agent Walker, can you keep Mrs Hirsh company?"

Walker said, "Of course, sir." Turning to Sarah, he said, "Please follow me."

Fleming and Simon followed Tanner into a nearby office. Once inside, Tanner said, "We have to discuss Rasputin. Simon, you have to give me more evidence and not just accuse him. He is the commander in chief; we cannot come to him with accusations without really strong evidence. What do you have for this?"

Simon said, "What I told you is everything I know; I will have to meet him in person."

Tanner said, "If he is really Rasputin, he will avoid meeting you; that's for sure."

Fleming said, "I have an idea. The president doesn't know what Simon looks like, so let's take a group of children around Simon's age on a tour at the white House. I will have my FBI representative there arrange the visit for this week

"That's a great idea," Tanner said. "We should move on it. So you will take care of it?"

"I will. Simon, what do you think?"

Simon said, "It's doable. He will not be expecting me. But it will be even better if you ask for an encounter with me specifically for another day, so he will definitely not expect me to be in that group. What do you think?"

Tanner said, "I think you're right. This way we can track him on two fronts."

Fleming said, "We have to take into consideration that if we are discovered, we will all be in trouble – I mean, Tanner and I, we will be fired."

"No, you won't," Simon said. "I see both of you in your posts for quite a few more years."

"That's comforting to know," Tanner said. "We have the advantage that we know and he doesn't. He is avoiding meeting Simon, but he has no idea at all that we know that."

Fleming said, "I will call now to arrange the tour for tomorrow afternoon. Tanner, you should call the president directly to ask him to meet Simon. He doesn't have to know about the tour, and he won't know, because he is not told about the day-to-day small things that go on in and around the White House."

Simon said, "All sounds good. Can we go now? My mother is waiting outside."

Tanner said, "You understand that all this is strictly top secret? No one outside the three of us can know. If anyone else finds out, he or she will be in danger, as will we."

"You mean my mother?" Simon asked.

Tanner said, "You guessed right. She will be in danger if she knows anything about this."

Fleming picked up his mobile phone and called the FBI representative at the White House. "Hi, it's me. Arrange a tour for schoolchildren at the White house for tomorrow afternoon."

She answered, "No problem, boss. I will call you back to confirm," and she hung up.

Fleming said to Tanner, "Now you just need to call the president and tell him that everything was successful and that you would like him to meet Simon. I think that he will find any kind of excuses to postpone the encounter."

Tanner said, "Yes, I will call him in thirty minutes. It will look odd if anyone notices that we both made calls almost at the same time."

Fleming called Agent Walker and Sarah over. They approached, and Fleming said, "Walker, take Mrs Hirsh and Simon back to their hotel. If there is anything new, we will advise. Maintain full security, 24/7."

Agent Walker said, "OK, boss, will do."

Fleming said, "Mrs Hirsh, I ask you to please do me a great favour and not leave the hotel for the next three days. Is this possible?"

Sarah asked, "Why? Is there a problem? Are we in some kind of danger? Does this have to do with the secret meeting you three just had?"

Fleming said, "Listen, we are just being cautious and trying to prevent all possible negative scenarios and keep you all in good health."

Sarah seemed convinced, and she and Simon followed Walker after saying goodbye. Thirty minutes later, they arrived at the hotel. Eric and Lilly were happy to see them. The whole floor in the hotel was reserved just for them and the FBI agents.

Tanner was still with Fleming when he made the phone call to the president. "Mr President, good afternoon. It's Tanner. We had a great morning, and the boy did exactly what he said he would. We are all in awe of that child."

The president said, "I am really impressed. Are we sure about him? I mean, is he safe for our country?"

"Of course, sir. He is an American-born citizen, and we know his entire history from A to Z and everything about his family for at least five generations. Would you like to meet him?"

"That would be great. I am excited to meet this genius kid. My secretary will check my schedule, and we will try for early next week. I am anxious. Well, Tanner, I am quite busy. We will talk then." He hung up before Tanner could get another word in.

Tanner said to Fleming, "He was very evasive. He sounded very interested in meeting Simon but was vague and said we should do it sometime next week. It's not like him to leave something for an undecided date."

Fleming said, "Anyone in the world would give anything to meet and talk with this human from another reality who has so many powers. Simon is the first ever of his kind, and I do not know if they will be another like him. I know now for sure that what Simon said about the president is true."

"How do we handle this?"

"We will have to handle this with extra care. We have to gather as many details as possible, and we do not have so many. We will have to involve three Republican senators and three congressmen and swear them to secrecy."

"That's a good idea, but we should also the Democrats, so it will not look like a conspiracy against the Democrats."

"How will we know that the senators and congressmen we choose are OK?" Fleming asked. "We should bring Simon to meet them. Anyway, we should choose elder lawmakers who have been around for a long time and in many administrations."

Fleming picked up his mobile phone and called Agent Walker. "Walker, are you at the hotel?"

Agent Walker replied, "Yes, sir."

"Bring Simon, without his mother, and meet us at our office at the Capitol. Act as if Simon is your son, and be very discreet. I will call Mrs Hirsh and explain."

"OK, sir, I will go now."

"Wait ten minutes, so I have time to call her," Fleming said and hung up.

He called Sarah next. "Hi, Mrs Hirsh. Sorry to disturb you, but there is a change in plans. I will need Simon for a couple of hours, and I will bring him back. It is very important. Walker will pick him up in ten minutes."

"Can I come with him?" Sarah asked.

"No, ma'am, it is very secret, but don't worry; Simon will be in no danger. Please continue to trust me. He is the most important VIP we have ever had to secure. We will guard him with our lives, I can assure you."

Sarah said, "Very well, I guess it's all right. Goodbye, Mr Fleming."

"Thank you and bye for now," Fleming replied.

At the hotel, there was a knock at the door. Jacob answered it. It was Agent Walker. "Hi again. I ..."

Before he could finish, Sarah came out of the room, and said, "Hi, Agent Walker. Simon will be ready in two minutes."

"I see that you spoke to my boss," he said. "I will bring him back as soon as we are done. From what I understand, it will take a couple of hours maximum."

Simon came out of a room. He was dressed in blue like a schoolboy of his age with a cap. He smiled and said, "Hi, Mr Walker. I am ready."

Agent Walker said, "Hi, Simon! Sorry to take you away so soon. The boss called and said that he urgently needs you in regard to what you know." To the rest of the family he said, "Have a great day."

Simon kissed his mother and Lilly and smiled at the others, and they left. Twenty minutes later they arrived at the Capitol. They went from the garage and through the back door directly to the FBI office. Fleming and Tanner were already there.

When they saw Simon, they smiled, and Tanner said, "We need you." Tanner turned towards Walker and the other three people in the office and said, "Please, all of you wait outside. Don't let anyone in without our approval, without exception."

172

As the four started to leave, Fleming said, "Wait, Walker." When the other three had left, he said, "Go and get Congressman McCarthy. Tell him to come to our office immediately. Tell him that it is a matter of national security and that he has to keep it to himself, nothing else."

Agent Walker said, "Yes, sir, right away," and he left.

Turning to Simon, Fleming said, "Regarding Rasputin, to uncover him, we cannot do it alone; it could be interpreted as a conspiracy. So Tanner and I have decided to involve three congressman and three senators from both political parties. Now, before we go forward, we will bring them here one by one, and—"

"I know," Simon interrupted. "You want me to make sure they are not in some way or another involved with Rasputin. I also thought about all this, but I did not know that you wanted to move immediately."

Fleming said, "This matter is the worst crisis of espionage we've ever faced, and we still do not know how wide and deep this infiltration is. Now, we mostly count on you."

There was a knock at the door. Tanner opened the door. Agent Walker was there with an older gentleman with long grey hair who was dressed in a British-made tailored tweed suit.

Tanner said, "Come in, Congressman McCarthy. You can leave us, Agent Walker."

Congressman McCarthy seemed a bit worried and obviously confused by this urgent meeting and the fact that the head of the CIA was in the FBI office. He asked, "What am I doing here? And what is the urgency?"

Tanner said, "Nothing to do with you. We just need your help."

As Congressman McCarthy came further into the office, he saw Fleming.

"Good afternoon, Congressman," Fleming said. "Sorry for the short notice, but we do have a very urgent matter. Please meet Sam, my nephew."

Simon extended his hand, and McCarthy shook it and said, "Nice to meet you, Sam."

Simon said, "Nice to meet you too." Looking at Fleming, he said, "I like this gentleman."

That made McCarthy smile, and he said, "I like you too."

Tanner and Fleming understood, so Tanner said, "Congressman, we are facing the worst-case scenario of spying within the government. There are spies at the highest spheres. We have to probe and find how bad the problem is. We need to know how many spies there are and discover who they are.

"So we are creating a small six-member coalition of congressmen and senators from both political parties. If we do this alone, it could look like a conspiracy against the government. So we are choosing the oldest congressmen and senators because of their experience and loyalty to the United States. Can you help us and guide us in choosing the other five?"

Congressman McCarthy said, "You can count on me, and I thank you for your trust. I recommend Congressman Davis from the Democratic Party and Jones from the Republicans. As to senators, you can call Collins and Ford from the Republicans and Jennings from the Democrats. Now this will not be enough without the attorney general."

Fleming said, "It's too early to talk to him. We will investigate first, and then we will move. For now this has to stay strictly secret; you cannot say anything to anyone but us."

Congressman McCarthy said, "You have my word, and please let me know when you can explain all the details."

Fleming said, "Thank you, Congressman, for your cooperation, and have a great day."

McCarthy left, and Fleming called Walker and gave the same instructions to call the next congressman. They repeated the same process for the other legislators. Simon did not go into the private parts of the legislators lives, just looking for security risks. He found nothing amiss. After they had finished with all six legislators, they were under less pressure; they could now count on six more people.

Fleming said, "Now we have to be ready for Simon's visit to the White House tomorrow. The tour will be made up of two five-year-old children from five different schools and one from another for a total of twelve children, Simon included.
Fleming:" can your people take care of picking up these children tomorrow"?

"No problem," Tanner replied. "What time?"

"Two o'clock at their respective schools. Here is the list and the names. I changed Simon's name to Robert Jennings. You will see his name in one of the schools. A woman by the name of Josie Donald will accompany the children to the White House. She is one of my agents from Milwaukee."

Fleming said, "So it will be better for her to be there to pick up the children. I will have a driver and a minibus go with your agent to pick them up. I will also get a permit for her to enter the White House. It's more normal for me to issue a permit than the CIA."

"OK, her name is on the list," Tanner said.

Fleming said, "Done. See you later."

Fleming took Simon with him and asked Walker to take him back to his mother. Thirty minutes later, Simon was back at the hotel. Now they had the rest of the day to be together as a family.

mon had to answer hundreds of questions from the family. He nswered just a few of the questions about the time travel. This four-and-a-half-foot child profoundly amazed the family with his great knowledge and power.

Simon had come to life as a blessing in disguise – not just for them but probably for humanity. But was humanity ready for him?

Sarah knew that something was bothering Simon. It probably had to do with the secret that always made their faces tense. Sarah was quite worried for Simon, despite all the assurances from Fleming and Tanner. She hoped that luck would keep Simon out of harm's way.

The Day of No Return

The next day would be a very special and unusual day. What would happen that day would change history in many ways. Simon woke up very early, around six o'clock. Something seemed to be bothering him. This was very unusual, as he almost never showed emotions. Even though he knew what was about to happen, he also knew that there were many dark facets related to Rasputin that were like wild cards. Who were all the spies? How many were there? And what were their roles in this spying ring?

Simon did not have a clear picture of the spying ring, and all these people were counting on him. It was a too-heavy responsibility on his shoulders. It was too big of a problem not just for him but also for everyone. His thoughts were those of an older man and not of Simon the child. He also had a gut feeling that something was going to go wrong, but he couldn't put his finger on what. All these worries prevented Simon from resting.

Simon left all the worries for later. Sarah was still asleep as he quietly went to take a shower. It was 7.20 a.m. He still had over an hour before Walker came to pick him up to take him to meet the scientists. The room was quiet and seemed relaxed, but his mind was not. He was already dressed when Sarah woke up.

Sarah said, "Good morning, darling. Why are you ready so early? Is something wrong?"

"No, Mom," Simon said. "I woke up early and couldn't stay in bed. I will call to get breakfast. Do you want some too?"

"Yes, I will take a shower and be ready in five minutes. Go ahead and order the usual, OK?" Sarah took a quick five-minute shower.

A few minutes later there was a knock at the door. Agent Walker said, "It's me, Mrs Hirsh, Agent Walker. Your breakfast is here."

Simon opened the door and said, "Good morning, Mr Walker. Would you join us for breakfast?"

Agent Walker said, "I already had breakfast, but I will accept a cup of coffee, thank you."

"Good morning, Mr Walker," Sarah said. "What is the schedule today?"

"I just know about this morning's meeting at the Library of Congress with the scientists. In the afternoon, Simon has to meet my boss."

"Am I allowed to come with Simon?" she asked.

"For the morning it's OK but not for the afternoon. Fleming and Tanner want to see Simon alone. Even I am not allowed."

By the time they finished breakfast it was already 8.35 a.m.

Sarah said, "We are ready when you are, Agent Walker."

Agent Walker said, "OK, let's go."

They left the room, and Sarah and Simon went to say hi to the kids and grandparents while Walker gave orders to the other agents to get the cars ready to leave. Ten minutes later, they had left the hotel.

At the Library of Congress security seemed heavier than usual. This time they entered through the parking lot. About a dozen FBI agents were waiting for them. They didn't leave anything to chance.

Sarah and Simon were escorted to the auditorium, where Fleming, Tanner, and a few scientists were already gathered.

Fleming said, "Good morning, Mrs Hirsh, and to you, Simon. We are a bit early; we are waiting for the rest of the scientists. Are you rested, Simon?"

178

Simon said, "Yes, I've been awake since six o'clock."

Discreetly Fleming took Simon to the side and asked, "Is there something bothering you? You seem worried."

Simon said, "There are some dark zones that I cannot foresee, and this situation with Rasputin has put a lot of pressure and responsibility on me. I hope that I can help to resolve this difficult situation."

Fleming said, "You are not alone. Do not forget that you are helping us beyond imagination. Without you, we would not have even discovered this terrible plot. Whatever happens from now on is our full responsibility. I am sure that everything will be fine."

At that moment, Tanning approached and said, "Everyone has arrived. Let's begin. We have to finish as soon as we can, so we can take care of our problem."

Walker took Sarah to take a seat, and Fleming, Tanner, and Simon took their places at centre stage.

One of the older scientists stood up and cleared his throat to get attention. He then said, "Good morning to you, Simon and gentlemen. I was chosen to speak for everyone in this auditorium regarding our voyage into the future. The results were beyond our wildest dreams. Simon, what you did was incredible. We have learned more than we have in the past hundred years and maybe all of our history. You really are a present from heaven."

Sarah was so proud. Tears dripped down her beautiful face.

"What you predicted for the next twenty years is more than real," the scientist continued. "We have analysed all the samples, tests, and readings. We will really do whatever is necessary to correct our path. It is not going to be easy. We will not be able to explain where we got our information or show the videos that we have taken. But we all promise to use all our influence and political everage to buy ourselves supporters to the reforms that we will push forward. The most difficult problem that we will face will be the energy lobby, or petroleum. The stakes are very high, and the taxes collected from petroleum are a very big income to our country and to most of the countries in the world."

Simon said, "I do understand, but this is the main item that you all have to work on. Your goal should be to create new solar energy. I will gladly help to find alternatives. Fossil fuel energies should be reduced by at least 20 per cent per year. This will also reduce our oil dependency by 20 per cent."

The scientist said, "Let's assume the US will adhere. What about other countries like Russia and China, all of Europe, etc.? What if they disagree?"

Simon said, "First, lobbying is very important. We will create a block of countries that want to save the planet. I am sure that Europe will follow, because they do not have oil wells. They will be easy. So all the green countries will join the battle.

"The green block will then boycott any product that comes from the non-green countries, mostly products that use any derivative of oil. It is feasible to cut fossil fuel usage 20 per cent per year without creating shortage problems or panic in the world. During this time we should push for solar and hydrogen technologies. Once these technologies are produced in mass, the cost will be reduced drastically, thus giving us an edge against non-clean systems. And for the first two years, we should increase the taxes on oil-derived products, cars, and industrial machinery.

"Most importantly, you scientists should prepare yourselves for a huge campaign of informing the public. Invite foreign scientists and try to convince them that the world as we know it will cease to exist in the span of twenty years. You got all the tools you need from our trip. Try to deduce the appropriate formulas from your results. Without your 100 per cent involvement, we will be facing the final phase of our planet. I am sure that you all agree with me."

They all nodded and murmured their agreement. Anyone looking at the scene without knowing the exact details would find it unreal and comical, all these world-renowned scientist deferring to and agreeing with this child.

The scientist speaking on behalf of everyone stood again and said, "If you do not mind, we have three more questions that we would like to ask you. We do not want to impose too much on you."

Simon said, "Please ask."

"First, can you enlighten us about the Bermuda Triangle? Second, how can we reduce world hunger? Third, do you care to comment on Darwin's theories? And sorry, a fourth one, how do you know so much and have so many powers when you are just a child?"

Simon smiled and said, "I will answer the questions in order of importance, starting with the last question.

"My childish appearance is totally irrelevant. What you see is not who I am inside. The world judges books by their covers. Of course in my case, it's a bit different. I am surrounded by an aura that is one million times wider and stronger than any of yours. For your knowledge, I am not just Simon and my father, David. When I came back to life and incorporated into this body, I brought with me over previous reincarnations. So my knowledge goes beyond your imagination. I draw information from the universal net.

"When I was teleported from paradise to this world, I went through a wrong channel. Because of this I am still connected to paradise, to a higher realm of existence. I am not sure if the Creator made a mistake, but I am sure that there must be a reason for this beyond my own comprehension. So I assume that my presence here in the world will have an end. I cannot predict when that end will be, but my being here creates and causes certain disturbances.

"For example, I cannot be near negativity or criminality. When I am in the presence of bad people and criminals, they are punished

181

n the spot, and I cannot do anything about it. I emit pure positive energy, which eradicates all negativity. The reason this does not happen around me very often is because I do have the four earthly elements, which in a sense limit the immediate eradication of negativity. I think first, and my reasoning is the tool for the final action. As you know, for every action there is a reaction.

"Now, coming to the second question, of how to reduce world hunger. Third World countries have very high birth rates and poor financial situations. All the men and women of these poor countries need sexual education. They have to be forced to take responsibility for their actions. These countries need to know that their citizens cannot have ten children, throw them to the streets, and expect the world to take care of them because of their poor sex habits.

"These countries should be denied help until they take their futures in their own hands and set a quota of no more than two children per family. They will have to create registries, and any family that bears more than two children will have their benefits cut.

"The IMF, World Bank, and similar institutions can hire water contractors to study and bring water to all cities and villages. These organisations should not grant cash to these countries, as not even 5 per cent gets to the needy.

"Many years ago, Israel taught these same people how to plant and grow fruits and vegetables in torrid areas with a minimum of water. They also taught them aquaculture for sources of protein from fish. But then the radical Islamists came and convinced the local governments to chase out the Israelis who had helped them so much. Today these same Islamists are the biggest part of these countries' problems. Facelift solutions will never work, and the problem will become bigger and bigger. All these villages should chase those murderers from their countries. As I said the first day we met, there needs to be a World War III to eradicate terrorism. It is the whole world's cancer.

"Villages should be taught how to grow their own vegetables and raise protein sources. When they have surpluses, they can even sell the food to the government to export it to other countries. This will slowly create their independence from other countries. This is the beginning of a world solution. Countries that will not cooperate should not receive the world's help.

"As to your third question, about Darwin's theories, they are theories, nothing else. Humans have evolved, but not as Darwin said. Our souls, or intelligence energies, are in fact extraterrestrial. When this energy comes to our world, it has to incorporate with the four earth elements – fire, air, water, and earth (dust). A soul can take form as a human, animal, plant, or mineral. Humans are the purest form and require a purer concentration of intelligence energy. Animals are the next purest and so on. The only evolution for the lower energies is in the form of food eaten by humans. Once ingested, these lower energies are incorporating into a higher energy for an eventual reincarnation. The same process is from higher to lower energy purity in a reincarnation. And thus allowing these lower energy once ingested by human allows this lower energies to reincarnate in a human body and the latter will facilitate their return onto a human form.(as i explain in the beginning in the tunnel of light that some reincarnations began separating from his essence).

"The only other types of evolution that come close to Darwin's theories are that people in different geographic locations look different and that there has been a big improvement from the caveman to today's man. People that lived in cold countries developed hairy bodies, and in very hot countries, the people had darker skin, hairless torsos, bigger feet, and so on. When people began travelling to different countries, their look also changed after generations and so on. But we did not come from the monkey; it was actually the other way around, as I just explained. We can upgrade or degrade from higher to lower and vice versa. So when a soul comes to this material world, depending on its level of pure energy, it could reincarnate into a monkey or anything else.

183

Now, for the first question. The Bermuda Triangle is due to an extraterrestrial city under the ocean floor. These extraterrestrial beings, or aliens, are different from other aliens in that they are or were humans like you all. This all happened 21,073 years ago. These beings were very advanced in technology, and as always, advanced means powerful. They subjugated other countries and races. They could travel through time and space. They had nuclear weapons a hundred times the strength of our nuclear bombs, and they enslaved many cultures, like the Egyptians and many other powerful peoples. They instilled fear and superstition to control the masses; their country was called Atlantis and was an island in the middle of the Bermuda Triangle.

"They became a very libertine society, Sodomy was part of their daily lives. They took slaves by force and used them for sex games. There were no laws and no protection for these poor slaves. The Atlanteans called themselves gods and invented names for themselves. Thousands of years later the Atlantean fake gods turned to myth and became the Greek Zeus, Apollo, Aphrodite, and so on. What lasted in the tales was the gods' brutality towards mortals and their pleasure in torturing and using them as sex slaves. Atlantis became Mount Olympus, supposedly in heaven, where these false gods lived.

"In fact these people invented a terrible weapon which attracted the sun's energy of over a million degrees Celsius. They did not have the right recipient for this heat, and the impact was worse than 500 nuclear bombs. They were so arrogant that they brought their own destruction. They defied the Creator, and this was the end of their world control.

"The island disintegrated and sunk to the bottom of the Bermuda Triangle. Some Atlanteans escaped, thanks to travelling in spaceships. They knew well the seabed, and their ships could also function as submarines. There were enormous cavities under the seabed, and they installed there a whole city with enormous generators to generate power and oxygen.

"During the thousands of years that followed, these survivors learned their lesson and dedicated themselves to preventing us from destroying our world again. Their physiognomies changed with the years. The need for sunlight turned their skin almost green, making them look as we describe extraterrestrials today. One of the reasons they appear and disappear suddenly from radar is that they emerge at a very high speed from the bottom of the sea and plunge as fast. But the reason they are still here is to keep an eye on our destructive technology and do everything in their power to stop us from destroying our green planet.

"One of the reasons that compasses malfunction and that many ships and planes get lost in the Bermuda Triangle is that the equipment these people have causes strong magnetic waves. I could extend largely on the matter, but it is not the moment.

"Many generations later, some cultures tried to imitate these sadists, as in the story of Sodom and Gomorra. Every time a new generation of dictators and criminals rises, they will be ultimately annihilated. The Creator watches over his creation, and that is probably the reason that I am here. Thank you."

All the people present stood up in a very loud round of applause. Sarah was elated and full of pride. Her eyes teared from happiness. Everyone applauded seemingly endlessly, for at least several minutes.

The scientists' representative requested permission to add one thing. After the applause subsided, he said, "Dear Simon, I think that I speak for all of us when I say thank you from the bottom of my heart for the wonderful lessons of technology and civility. We also thank Mrs Hirsh for having such a wonderful being. Thank you."

There was another round of applause until Fleming and Tanner took Simon to the back office. Fleming asked Walker to take Sarah to the hotel. It was one thirty at time to get ready for the visit at the White House with the other children.

The White House Visit

Not long after two o'clock the minibus of children arrived at the Library of Congress. Two young ladies directed the group of children on a tour of the world-famous Library of Congress, giving information about the building to the young audience.

Fleming was still with Simon and said, "Simon, go ahead and join the children. Blend in, and try to find a friend that you can sympathise with. I will act as if I don't know you in front of these kids. My agent is the young blonde woman. She will keep an eye on you. If there is something really urgent, talk to her very discreetly. I will advise then."

Simon nodded, and as soon as the group of children arrived by him, he melded in with the youngsters of his age and the same approximate height. Now Fleming could barely notice him. Fleming smiled and waited until the children had finished their short visit and got back on the bus.

Now the very delicate mission had begun. Fleming crossed his fingers and prayed for the success of his hardest mission ever. He took out his mobile phone and called Tanner, who was having his men follow all known Russian agents and listen to their transmissions, looking for anything out of the ordinary.

In view of the seriousness of the situation, 300 CIA agents were involved in this mission and countless FBI agents. This was the worst crisis that the nation was facing.

The minibus arrived at the gate of the White House. A security officer entered the bus. One of the young women showed him a list with all the children's names and her ID, and the other woman followed suit. The officer checked the entire bus while outside two other security officers checked under the bus with mirrors at the end of long metal poles. Once the security check ended, the children were allowed inside the main gate. The blonde woman departed first, followed by the children two by two and the second woman at the end.

The children, despite their young age, were excited to be at the residence of the president of the United States; they all watched TV and know everything about the White House and who the president was.

As they walked through the hallways, their guide explained the history of each and every room and of every portrait of all the past presidents. They arrived at the Oval Room, and she explained that this room was where the president met with foreign presidents, prime ministers, kings, and so on. She said, "If we are lucky, we will see the president when he is free."

Just then two Secret Service agents came and stood just outside the Oval Room, one on each side of the door. One said into his earpiece, "John in position," and the other said, "Marcus in position." The president was probably about to leave the room. The guide asked the children to move back about 10 yards, which they did. A few minutes later, the president came out, followed by the secretary of state and his chief of staff.

The president asked, "What do we have here?" as he looked at the cute little children staring at him in awe. He smiled and said, "Good afternoon, children. I am glad to have such a nice visit today." He continued talking, and no one noticed Simon looking at him strangely, as if scanning him. The president continued, "You are all the future of this great nation of ours. Who knows, maybe one of you could be the future president. Thank you all for coming. Bye, kids, and be well."

The small group continued the tour around the building. When an hour had passed, their guide said, "We were lucky to have seen the president, and now it's about time for you to go back home to your parents."

hey group returned to the bus. One of the two women counted the children as they boarded. They were all accounted for. Simon seemed lost in his thoughts as the bus drove off. Every child was taken home feeling happy to have visited the White House. They had stories to tell their families and friends.

Simon's stop was saved for last because they were afraid of being followed and did not want to jeopardise the operation. Simon was dropped off in the bus parking lot, where Fleming was waiting for him. Fleming then drove Simon to the FBI head office. Simon did not say a word during the trip. Fleming looked at him silently. It seemed that this child carried the whole world on his little shoulders.

Once at Fleming's office, Simon was given other clothes to change into. Nothing was taken lightly. The Russians might have people inside the Bureau. Simon sat in front of Fleming, and at that moment there was a knock at the door. It was Tanner.

Fleming said, "Just in time, Tanner. Please take a seat." Tanner did so, and Fleming continued, "Well, Simon, by your look, it seems that things are bad. Can you tell us?"

Simon said, "I did meet the president in person, and the infiltration is very deep and very bad."

"Did you find out who else is involved?" Tanner asked.

Tanner and Fleming were sitting on the edge of their seats. Worry and a million questions were painted all over their faces, and they were hanging on to Simon's every word.

Simon said, "There are nine people inside the White House who are directly connected to Rasputin, who receives orders directly from the Kremlin. The nine people are the secretary of state, the White House chief of staff, the secretary of defence, the president's personal secretary, his two personal body guards, the attorney general, and the head of the Secret Service."

Fleming said, "But that is impossible. How did he get spies into all those key positions?"

Tanner said, "Simon, it doesn't make sense. How can all the top-ranking people have chosen to betray their country?"

Simon said, "First, the president chose all the people to fill these positions. Second, if you investigate these nine people, you'll find they're all twins, like our president. The rest you know; the same procedure was used, and at the age of eighteen or so the abducted twins took their US twins' places.

"They engaged in politics and backed each other up at the Democratic conventions. They're brilliant and charismatic. They had the best professors, and they never spoke in Russian, to avoid having an accent or accidentally slipping into Russian in a conversation. They are real Americans for everything, but their loyalty is to Russia."

Fleming said, "You make sense, but this is the worst espionage case of this country ever. Is there something you can do to eliminate this threat?"

Simon said, "If they were murderers, yes, they would die if I met them, but in this case they have done no crime, at least not by the supreme justice. In this case the crime is political, punishable by man. I do not have the power to kill, but heaven acts through me in the presence of murderers. It is as if they are coming to the highest court and being judged accordingly. Through me a tunnel from heaven stays open."

Tanner said, "We should investigate this matter before we make any move that could cost us our heads."

Fleming said, "Go ahead if you want, but I will begin planning our next move. I trust Simon's revelations. Until now he has not failed once."

189

Tanner said, "Well, let's move simultaneously then. We should keep in contact twenty-four hours a day."

Fleming said, "OK, I will send Simon to his hotel." He called Agent Walker and said, "Get the squad ready to take Simon to the hotel, and then come here."

A few minutes later Walker stepped in. "Hi, boss. We are ready." He turned to Simon. "Hi, Simon. Are you ready to go?"

Simon said, "Hi, Agent Walker. Yes, I am ready."

Walker and Simon walked out, under the worried gaze of Fleming and Tanner.

Fleming said, "Tanner, look at this kid, not even six years old, and he has more intelligence than those 100 scientists all together. If not for him, imagine what would have happened with this unprecedented spy case and all the other cases. I am afraid even to imagine the devastating effects this would have caused."

Tanner said, "I agree, but now I am worried about the future. We have to involve the six legislators now. We cannot waste more time. You are right; Simon has never failed in his predictions or analysis. Let's move now."

"OK, I will ask the senators and congressmen to meet us today." Fleming picked up the phone and called the six senators and congressmen. They agreed to meet at the Library of Congress in two hours after he said, "It's a matter of national security of the highest importance."

***

As Agent Walker and Simon drove to the hotel, Walker noticed that three cars were following him. He radioed the agents in the three other FBI cars, and they moved in a matter of seconds to cover Agent Walker's car. They tried to identify the cars following them, but suddenly the three cars changed course and disappeared in different directions.

The FBI cars stopped in formation. Walker said to the others, two agents per car, "I am positive that they were following us."

One of the other agents replied, "Maybe not. Maybe just a coincidence?"

Agent Walker said, "No, I am sure because the three cars disappeared once you guys came to back us up. There are no coincidences in our business. Let's move with the utmost vigilance."

They continued their trip towards the hotel; they were just about a mile away. Walker called the agents in the hotel and told them to be on alert and to prepare for Simon's arrival.

The four FBI cars entered the hotel's parking lot. Once there, eight fully armed agents were waiting. The agents immediately surrounded Simon as he exited the car and led him to the elevators. They escorted him all the way to his room, where his mother and siblings were waiting; Walker had notified Sarah of their arrival.

Sarah was anxious from waiting. Seeing Simon, she smiled and relaxed. She kissed him, and Eric and Lilly also greeted him warmly. Simon had become a hero to them, even though him being like both a brother and a father was so confusing for them. The grandparents joined them. The FBI urged them to enter the suite and not gather in the hallway, so the grandparents quickly entered the room.

Agent Walker called Fleming and told him about the three cars that had followed them almost to the hotel. Fleming was furious and worried at the same time. He asked Tanner if his people had followed the FBI cars, but Tanner answered negatively.

leming asked, "Do you think that Rasputin's people have discovered our plans?"

"How?" Tanner asked. "We have been very careful. I do not think that it was really important, just a coincidence. We have checked, and each of the cars went a different way. There is no evidence that they were connected."

Fleming said, "Well, for now, let's forget about it. In one hour our the congressmen and senators will be here, and the spy ring will be a hard item to sell."

At the hotel, the family gathered around Simon and tried to understand what was going on and why there was so much secrecy.

Simon seemed worried and said, "I cannot say anything, but I am helping the authorities in various situations that are very delicate."

Sarah said, "But, darling, you look worried and very tired."

Sarah's mother said, "Come eat, darling; you must be starved."

Simon smiled and said, "Oh, yes, I am hungry!" He ran to the dining room. The table was garnished with various types of food, but Simon went straight to the fries and hamburgers and ate as if it were his last meal.

The phone rang, and Sarah answered it. "Yes?"

"Hi, Mrs Hirsh. This is Fleming speaking."

"Hi, Mr Fleming, how are you?"

"Sorry to bother you," Fleming said, "but we do need Simon immediately. Walker is there, and he will pick him up in ten minutes. Sorry."

"Simon is exhausted, and he is having lunch. Can he rest a bit?"

"OK, let's make it in half an hour. It is really very important."

"OK, I will tell him. Bye, Mr Fleming," she said and hung up, feeling a bit upset. She could barely spend time with Simon anymore. Since he'd been born, she'd known that this would happen, without knowing to what extent.

At the other end, Fleming and Tanner were waiting. The congressmen and senators arrived before Simon. Fleming and Tanner greeted them, but their faces were grave, with poor smiles on their lips.

Fleming said, "Thank you, gentlemen, for attending this very special, ultra-secret meeting. Please take a seat. As I instructed you at our first meeting, no one knows that we are here. Gentlemen, what we are about to tell you today is very sad news for our country.

"We have known each other for decades, and we chose the six of you because we know that you are the heart of this country and that this country is your highest priority. I will let Mr Tanner, who has been the head of the CIA for the past twelve years, explain the gravity of this situation."

Tanner said, "Congressmen, Senators, to be blunt, the highest spheres of our government have been penetrated by a group of master spies."

The legislators all looked at each other as if this was beyond comprehension, some kind of unthinkable catastrophe, as if extraterrestrials had landed.

Tanner continued, "You all are or where once in the security committees. You have heard about the master spy Rasputin and also about this miraculous child Simon?"

They all nodded. Tanner proceeded to explain and present files on the LCD giant screen installed for this purpose. He showed

193

the birth certificates of each of the Russian spies, leaving the president for the end. The congressmen and senators were all ears and kept nodding or moving their heads. They mumbled occasionally, probably curses like "sons of bitches."

At that moment Walker and Simon entered. Fleming made a sign for Walker to leave and gestured to Simon to come next to him, which he did. Fleming said, "This is Simon." All said hi and looked at Simon curiously, very interested. Fleming explained Simon's deeds, the success of the voyage to the future, and how Simon had come to find out about the spy ring.

One of the senators said, "This is a very grave accusation, and it seems unreal. What if you are wrong?"

Tanner said, "Please look at the screen. These are all the files. We have analysed the DNA of the babies that were left at the hospital – blood tests and so on. We managed to get samples of the suspects' DNA. Their DNA is very similar to the DNA of the babies left at the hospital, because they are identical twins, but there are clear differences. These people are not the original twins that grew up in the United States until university, when they were replaced by the Russian twins. In all cases someone contacted them, and then they disappeared silently, without anyone noticing."

One of the congressmen said, "This sounds like a farfetched spy movie and too incredible. It makes it very hard to believe. They are the most powerful people of this administration. What do you want to do exactly, and what do you expect us to do?"

Fleming said, "You haven't heard the worst part of it: who Rasputin is. I will let Simon explain. He might look like just a defenceless child, but he has astonished our entire scientific community, and his knowledge overrides all of theirs, combined."

Simon stood and looked at all of them. Finally he said, "Rasputin is the president."

They were all shocked and couldn't believe their ears. They stood up and protested, especially the Democrats. One of the congressmen exclaimed, "This is a defamation of the Democratic Party. I do not want to hear more. I am leaving."

Simon calmly took the congressman by the hand and motioned him to sit down, which he did. They all calmed down and curiously watched the scene. Simon whispered something in the congressman's ear. The congressman's eyes opened very wide, and he said, "How can you know that?"

Simon repeated the same ritual with the other five legislators, who all had the same reaction. Then Simon went back to his place facing all of them and said, "I told you all very intimate information that no one but you knows, not even your wives or families. There is no doubt about this information, as you can all verify this information individually. So you can be sure that this is not a partisan plot. This is just about the security of your country; partisanship has nothing to do here. Now time is of the essence."

One of the senators asked, "So what are your plans? How are you going to handle this? Mr Tanner and Mr Fleming, you are the heads of your departments, and in a way, without finger-pointing, you are the ones responsible for this impossible situation."

One of the congressmen asked, "Why doesn't Simon resolve this dangerous situation as he did with the terrorists in Canada?"

Simon said, "Mr Fleming and Mr Tanner asked me the same thing. As I told them, I cannot kill people by will. I am an open tunnel between heaven and earth, and when I am in the presence of real murderers, heaven acts, because evil cannot survive near a divine environment. In this case these spies have not killed anyone. Heaven does not get involved in politics, and I have no rights to get involved in their removal."

Tanner said, "We will have to arrange for individual accidents. We cannot have everyone killed at the same place and time."

Fleming said, "I prefer that we take them alive and use unclaimed corpses from the morgue to make it seem that they are dead. This way, we can get answers from them, but there will still be bodies for the burials. They will receive all the honours possible so they will remain in good standing in the public's eye. We can blame terrorists in some of the cases."

One of the senators said, "But in the autopsies they will discover that they are not the people that we said they were."

Fleming said, "No worries there. Since they're from the federal government, the FBI will carry out the investigation, and by the same token, the legal forensic department will be from the FBI."

Tanner said, "Of course it is obvious that you cannot say a word about this operation, not even to your pillow. We will call it Operation Eagle 1."

Fleming said, "That's a good name for it." All of them nodded in approval.

One of the congressmen said, "I am happy we're going to avoid killing anyone and also glad that no one will know about these spy infiltrations to the highest positions in our government. We could have been the ridicule of all nations, especially our intelligence community. Where will you keep them locked up?"

Tanner said, "We have a secret prison, and they will never see the light of day again."

Fleming took out a Bible and asked everyone to raise his hand and swear to keep the secret forever, which they all did without protest. This was too big. They had found a good solution to this terrible situation, and now they had to prepare for this operation.

Tanner said, "We will have to start with the president first, so he will not replace the supposedly dead spies with his own people. The vice president will become president. He is not a spy, so

Rasputin will not be a problem any longer. The president will have to be eliminated and not taken alive; there's no other way to do it. He is always surrounded by Secret Service, so the kill will have to be at the White House or in a conference."

A senators said, "There is a banquet for handicapped children the day after tomorrow. The president is to be the guest of honour and the speaker. You can make your move then."

Tanner said, "We will take care of it."

"How?" asked a congressman.

"Don't worry," Tanner said. "We will find a way that will not raise eyebrows."

Fleming said, "Let's go now, and may G-d help us."

They all answered amen, and the legislators left.

Fleming then told Simon, "You did good, Simon, when you spoke to each one individually. I am sure that what you told them was very intimate. That was a good and smart move; it convinced them that you were right about everything we said."

Tanner said, "Well, let's leave now and begin Operation Eagle 1."

Fleming called Walker and asked him to take Simon to his family and to be vigilant. They all left in different directions. On the way to the hotel, three black cars again followed Walker from far away. The FBI drivers noticed the cars and radioed Walker. Minutes later all three cars stopped and then disappeared.

Walker called Fleming. "Boss, I know now for sure that it was no coincidence. This is the second time three cars have followed us. Once we communicated between FBI cars, they stopped and disappeared in different directions. It might be the Russians. Maybe they have doubts and are trying to find out what we are doing?"

Fleming said, "I don't know, but you have to be careful with Simon's security. We will give him two days' rest."

"OK, boss, we will. Bye." Walker hung up and turned to Simon. "Simon, you have two days' rest."

Simon said, "Well my family will be happy, especially Lilly. I guess that it will be good." Simon was never enthusiastic. He rarely laughed or played. He was always serious and thinking about serious subjects.

A few minutes later, they arrived at the hotel. As usual, security was tight, especially after being followed for the second time. Simon went back to his family and told them that he had two days to be with them without interruption.

Agent Walker asked, "Do you all need anything?"

They asked for movies and all kind of sweets and food. They were tired of hotel food.

Sarah asked, "Can we all go out for shopping or just to visit a museum?"

Agent Walker said, "Sorry, Madam, but I have strict orders to keep you here for security reasons, your security. We have to be sure of some things before you can go out normally again."

"Is there a problem that I should know about?" she asked.

"Nothing specific; we are just taking precautions. Well, I will have your needs taken care of, and if you need me, I will be nearby."

"Thank you, Agent Walker," Sarah said. "Bye for now."

Walker left, and two agents remained outside the door. Forty-five minutes later, there was a knock at the door, and Sarah opened it. It was an agent bringing all kinds of sweets and about a dozen movies. The kids were happy, but not Simon, who seemed to be lost in his thoughts.

The grandparents were playing gin rummy, and Sarah sat down to watch a movie with Eric and Lilly. Sarah asked, "Simon, want to watch this Disney movie with us?"

Simon said, "No, Mom, I am sleepy; I'm going to lie down for a bit."

"What's wrong, darling?"

"Nothing. I simply want to rest for a while." He went and lay down in his room, which was interconnected to this main room.

The family spent two days in the rooms without leaving. They had just shorts visits with Agent Walker and room service, always with an FBI escort. The agents were on high alert.

At 11.20 a.m. on Monday, Dan and Jacob were watching a baseball game when suddenly the game cut out and "Breaking News" flashed on the TV.

"Sarah, come fast!" Dan shouted. "There is an urgent announcement."

Sarah came running, followed by Simon.

A man reporting from a Hilton Hotel said, "At a humanitarian conference at this Hilton Hotel, the president of the United States suffered a heart attack and was immediately taken to the Hospital in critical condition. We have no word yet about his current condition."

Sarah said, "Oh my G-d, the president might die."

Dan said, "I hope that he will be OK. We will pray for his well-being."

The family joined him in his prayers and well wishes. Simon watched the news without showing any emotions.

As the adults discussed the report, "Breaking News" again flashed on the screen. The report cut to hundreds of cameramen and news people waiting in front of a podium. A man in a white shirt, the chief of surgery of the Mount Sinai Hospital, came out and said, "The president suffered a massive stroke and heart attack. We did everything we could, but he passed away at 11.45 a.m. We all pray and give our condolences to his family and to the nation."

Fleming was standing next to the doctor, and he took the microphone and said, "I am FBI Director Fleming. We all pray for the president's family; may he rest in peace. We have investigated, and there is no evidence of foul play. Though he was just forty years old, he had a very severe heart attack. At this moment the vice president is being advised and prepared to be sworn in as the next president of the United States of America."

Simon thought, *Operation Eagle 1 has begun.* Sarah and her parents and in-laws were crying in silence. It was terrible and very sad news for the United States and the world. For a moment Sarah looked at Simon; he looked like an ice statue, frozen with no emotions.

There was a knock at the door, and Eric opened it. It was Agent Walker and two other agents. Their eyes were red, and Agent Walker had difficulty speaking as he asked Sarah, "Have you heard?"

Sarah said, "Yes, it is so sad. He was so young and handsome." She let out a hysterical cry, and her mother brought her a glass of water.

Simon looked at Walker and the other agents. They did not know a thing about Operation Eagle 1. Simon was not happy about the killing of the president, but there had been no other solution. This was the best way out of this situation. They had cut the head off the snake. The other spies would have to stay put until they received new orders directly from the Kremlin. Fleming and Tanner would have a harder task after the second "accident." Simon was sure that they would take care of the others in different ways, but the Kremlin would still quickly find out that the Americans knew about Rasputin. They probably already suspected it, but they wouldn't move yet, because they would not be sure how much the Americans knew.

In Moscow, the news came as a heavy blow. These operations had taken over thirty-five years and cost billions of dollars. They had been very hopeful of succeeding in the deepest spy ring ever. In a way, they could have controlled the United States of America without shooting one bullet. The head of the Russian intelligence agency suspected that this had something to do with the genius child, Simon. They had to find a solution to this problem. That meant a not-good forecast for Simon. Now he and his family were in real danger.

The President's Funeral

It was a silent and sad day in America. People had cried a lot, and some were still crying. The country was in mourning, but it was a bright and shining morning, and it was a great victory for the American intelligence community. Fleming and Tanner had successfully eliminated the Rasputin menace. Now they had to keep an eye on the others and patiently wait for the right moment.

The phone rang at three o'clock, and Jacob answered it. "Hello?"

"Good afternoon. This is Mr Fleming. With whom am I speaking?"

"This is Jacob Hirsh. How are you, sir?"

"As well as I can be. May I speak to Mrs Sarah Hirsh?"

"Of course, sir, just a minute." He went and called Sarah.

Sarah took the phone and said, "Hi."

"Hello, Mrs Hirsh, it's Fleming. I guess that you have heard the terrible news?"

"Yes, I did. It's terrible."

"Yes, it is," Fleming said. "I would like to ask you to let Simon come to the Capitol. We need him over here. Walker will be there in thirty minutes. Is that OK with you?"

"Simon will be delighted; he is like a lion in a cage. It's OK with me, and he will be ready. Bye, Mr Fleming." She hung up then called out, "Simon, Mr Fleming called; he is sending Agent Walker to pick you up in thirty minutes."

Simon said, "OK, I will go get dressed."

Sarah noticed a sign of satisfaction on his face. It was rare to see him act like a child. He enjoyed being with adults.

"Simon, can I ask you a question that is bugging me?" Sarah asked.

Simon said, "Yes, and I will answer if I can."

"Do you know anything about the president's death?"

"Mom, I've been here without moving for the past two days." Simon could not lie, so he just stated a fact without directly denying his involvement.

Sarah was not duped but did not push the subject further. She kept her doubts to herself, but fear invaded her entire being. Looking at Simon, she tried to chase these terrifying thoughts out of her mind.

Simon was ready by the time they heard a knock at the door. Dan opened the door. It was Agent Walker and two other agents. "Hi, Agent Walker, gentlemen," Dan said.
Agent Walker said to Simon, "Fleming needs you. He asked me to pick you up."

Simon said, "Yes, I know. He called here too. I am ready."

Simon and the agents headed downstairs. In the elevator Simon felt that something was wrong. Once they were out of the elevator, Simon took Walker to the side and said, "These two have betrayed us."

Walker turned around with his gun pulled out, but the other two FBI agents already had their guns out and shot Walker, wounding him and leaving him for dead. Simon was about to kill both of them, but one had a Visio- phone and said, "Look here, your sister and brother are at our mercy."

On the screen Lilly and Eric were blindfolded and saying, "Simon, don't come. Don't worry about us."

Simon couldn't see who their captors were. They had done that so Simon couldn't kill all of them at once. Simon would not risk jeopardising the lives of his siblings, or his children.

The shorter of the two agents pushed Simon inside the car. Simon looked over at Walker; he knew that Walker was only wounded and not dead. The agents sped away quickly, the wheels squeaking on the parking floor and leaving a trail of smoke behind them. The second agent covered Simon's eyes with a bandana. They were afraid of what he could do because they had been in Canada and knew many more things. They knew how Simon could be partially neutralised. They never spoke between them, writing messages instead. They never mentioned any names, and they had a type of small beeper that created distortional sound waves to confuse Simon and prevent him from detecting them.

Simon asked, "Why are you doing this, betraying your country?"

The agent who had showed him the video said, "Why wars? Why killings? Why thousands of casualties in Iraq? One word: money. The whole world revolves around money. Believe me; we have 100 million reasons." The two laughed sarcastically.

"What will you do with me?" Simon asked.

"You will see soon enough," the agent replied. "I know that you could have killed us, and you still can, but if we do not call every fifteen minutes and give a code, your brother and sister will be killed. So don't try anything. As long as you cooperate, everything will be OK."

They drove for twenty-five minutes and then suddenly stopped. Simon heard a gate opening, and the car moved again. He could hear the sound of tires on gravel. He tried to see, but his eyes were covered tightly with the bandana, and his hands were tied behind his back. His real concern was Lilly and Eric. He had to think of how to free them without them being harmed.

The car stopped, and the doors were opened. Some people outside the car greeted the agents in English but with heavy foreign accents. Simon knew right away that they were Iranians. These traitors were betraying their country by selling him to the Iranians. He could have sensed that if he hadn't been so preoccupied with worry for Eric and Lilly. He had been sure that it was the Russians; that would have made more sense, because of the Rasputin spy ring.

The moment Simon stepped out of the van, the skies darkened. Everyone looked up, not understanding what was happening. The two agents got very worried, because they knew what Simon was capable of. They all rushed inside the embassy building.

The two agents requested their final payment. They wanted to leave as fast as possible. They were really worried for themselves. They had been planning this betrayal for the past three weeks. They had told their families that they had received a new assignment and were being transferred to Brazil. They had already sent their families there after telling them not to tell anyone, not even their parents, where they were going, with the pretence that the new assignment was top secret.

An Iranian foreign agent had found them through a common acquaintance and contacted them with an offer to make $100 million per person, not telling them what they would have to do. The idea of being rich had slowly worked itself into their minds. Greed slowly had taken over, and the little remorse they had still had disappeared. They had met with the Iranian. When they'd heard his request, they had said, "No way! You want our deaths?" But the Iranian had been convincing and had given each of the rogue agents an advance of $100,000. They had never seen so much money at one time and had agreed to the offer. The Iranians then had paid each of them $50 million, wired to accounts in the Cayman Islands opened for this purpose.

Now that they had delivered the package, the Iranians transferred the rest of the payment to each. The agents verified the transaction by computer and were satisfied. They shook hands and left the room, leaving Simon, still tied up but no longer blindfolded, behind.

They were counting on the Russians being suspected in Simon's kidnapping, because they could have found at Simon's powers. They also had faked their own deaths. They had burned different bodies in two different locations so they could not be identified, but they had buried a few clues – like a badge, a watch, and a few other items – nearby so they could be found.

Simon was put in an electrified metal cage with 50,000 volts running through it. It was so narrow that if Simon extended his small arms, he would be electrocuted. The agents had explained Simon's powers to the Iranians and had told them to prevent him from extending his arms. Simon sat in a wooden chair in the cage. The chair was on top of a wooden platform, so he could put his feet down and not get electrocuted, but his feet were too short to touch the bottom anyway.

Simon's face did not show any emotions. He looked serene, and that worried the Iranians. He scrutinised each person present, which froze their inner beings. His eyes had a fiery look, as if he was about to burst, but his face did not show any grim or nervous tics. The Iranians left the room, leaving Simon with two guards.

The Iranians took the FBI agents' car inside a covered garage and began taking it apart to be able to make it disappear. Meanwhile the two agents got into the diplomatic car that was to take them to a private airport, where an Iranian diplomatic jet would be waiting to fly them to Brazil.

The gates of the embassy opened to let the car out. The windows were heavily tinted to hide the car's interior and occupants. The car drove out, the gate closing behind them. After they had driven just 300 yards, various cars formed a blockade, and two dozen armed agents came out and surrounded the Iranian car, prepared to shoot at the first move. The two traitors, who were in the back, killed the other passengers and the driver and came out shouting,

"It's us! Don't shoot! The Iranians were holding us prisoner. Don't shoot." They came out without weapons with their hands up, as was usual in situations like this.

A few agents pushed them against the car, and one said, "Hands on top of the car, and spread your legs."

One of the two traitors screamed, "Hey! It's us. What are you doing?"

The agents shook them down for weapons and all their belongings, and put everything in two separate plastic bags. Inside the car they found the three dead bodies. The two traitors continued claiming their anger over their treatment. At that moment Fleming came out of one of the cars and walked towards them as they were being handcuffed.

He said, "Don't bother yourselves; we know everything. Your accomplices were caught, and the kids are free. Walker is just wounded, and he told us what really happened. You pieces of shit, all this for money. You have betrayed your country." To the agents he said, "Get this garbage out of my sight, and I want them to get the treatment I have reserved for them."

Turning back to the traitors, he said, "Simon is inside, I presume?"

The traitors told him that Simon was in a high-voltage cage, and then they were put in one of the FBI cars. More troops arrived and surrounded the Iranian embassy. Many blocks around the embassy had been evacuated.

Fleming pulled out a card with the Iranian embassy's number and called them from his mobile phone. After three rings a man at the embassy answered and said in an heavy accent, "The Iranian embassy, hello?"

Fleming said, "I am the director of the FBI. Who am I speaking with?"

The man at the embassy said, "I am Ahmed Buthro, secretary of His Excellence Idris Bajian Jenad. How can I help you?"

"I want to speak with the ambassador immediately."

"He is in a conference in his office; call later," Ahmed said.

"Are you really an idiot or just acting like one? We have the embassy surrounded. You are holding a young child hostage. If he is not released in fifteen minutes, we will attack the embassy. Now go tell the ambassador, whatever his name is. The clock is ticking."

There was silence for a few seconds, and then Ahmed said, "One moment please," and put Fleming on hold.

Two minutes later, a new man said, "Hello, sir. My name is Jeha Ben Jabar. I am head of security for the embassy. What can I do for you?"

Fleming said, "Listen, whoever you are, you have eleven minutes to free the child. If not, we are coming in. Ten minutes left."

Jeha said, "You seem to forget that we are in a sovereign territory, and you have no rights whatsoever!"

Fleming said, "Seven more minutes."

The Iranians began worrying, and finally the ambassador came to the phone and said, "This is the ambassador, and if you attack the embassy, you will regret it. No one will survive this attack."

Fleming heard people shouting, "Allahu Akbar! Allahu Akbar!" in the background, and he ordered his men, "Now! Blow the gate!" There was a big boom, and the gate broke in pieces.

At that moment inside the embassy, the people guarding Simon strung cables between Simon's body and the cage. The ambassador gave the orders to go ahead, and they flipped the main switch to electrify the cage. Simon began to shake violently, and smoke and sparks shot out of Simon's body and within and around the cage. Suddenly the whole embassy began burning, and inside the people ran for their lives.

Outside, the sky darkened, and a big whirlpool of fire came down on the embassy. Fleming and his people quickly retreated a few hundred yards away. Fleming was happy that he'd moved all the surrounding neighbours. A big explosion occurred from within the embassy. Military trucks and a lot of soldiers closed off the entire neighbourhood. Fleming called the new president and explained what was happening. News vans showed up, and helicopters, military and civil, hovered overhead but could not get too close. A column of fire and a very bright light came down on the embassy, turning it to just dust.

Tanner arrived and joined Fleming. They retreated some more, watching the scene through binoculars. Fleming had tears in his eyes, unable to contain them. He was thinking of Simon. He loved this special child that was no more. Fleming explained to Tanner what had transpired in the past few hours.

All the TV stations were showing what was happening, and officials were instructing everyone to stay as far away as possible. Of course no one had any idea what was happening or what whirlpool of fire coming down from heaven was.

At the hotel Sarah was dead concerned about Simon. She waited impatiently for news from Fleming, but the phone did not ring. She and the grandparents hugged Lilly and Eric with all their strength, as if protecting them. The ordeal her children had gone through was too much for her. She was grateful to Agent Walker, who, even though wounded badly, had the presence of mind to call his boss, who had moved quickly and freed Eric and Lilly.

Walker was out of danger. If he had not been wearing a bulletproof vest, the second bullet would have killed him. The bullet that had hit him in the neck should have easily killed him.

Simon must have done something before being pushed in the car; he was sure of it. Simon had probably saved his life. He was really concerned about this little child whom he'd learned to like and respect. He was amazed by Simon's capacities and found him to be a very likeable individual.

He picked up his cell and called Fleming. "Hello, sir. This is Walker."

"Walker! Are you OK?" Fleming asked.

"I will be, but what is happening now? Is Simon okay?"

Fleming hesitated for a few seconds and then told Walker what had happened since he had passed out after being wounded.

After some hesitation, Agent Walker asked in a trembling voice, "And ... Simon?"

Fleming took a deep breath and said, "He is no more, and I have not told his ... Oh my G-d! Walker, I will call you back."

Fleming hung up and took out his binoculars. He could not believe his eyes. From the middle of the fire and the rubble where the embassy had been, a human form, or what looked like one, was coming out. It was Simon. He was surrounded by fire as he walked slowly forward. His eyes were blood red. He was at the centre of a whirlpool of a very bright light. Suddenly the heavens lit up, and the whirlpool began expanding and widening by the minute. Beings of light started coming out of the column of now-gigantic proportions. The column extended for miles into the air, straight up to the heavens. They could not see the end of it. The light beings dove down towards the earth at high speeds. Every time a light being passed close to the crowds, some people fell down to the ground and disintegrated totally, leaving a pile of dust.

Fleming ran towards Simon, as close as he could, and shouted into a megaphone, "Simon! Simon, please stop all this destruction! We are your friends! Please, Simon!"

A strange, rough voice came out of Simon's lips as if coming out of the depths of hell: "I cannot stop; it's not me but heaven. Humans have broken lose the gates between heaven and earth. Judgment Day has begun."

Fleming asked, "But why us? We are your friends! What can we do? What should we do? Please, Simon, help us!"

"I wish I could. Please tell Sarah, Eric, and Lilly that I loved them."

Simon then walked away, the whirlpool following him. Now it had become at least a mile wide. All the sky seemed to be on fire. It really was the end of the world.

Fleming called two of the agents at the hotel and asked them to bring Sarah to him immediately. He then called Sarah. As soon as she picked up, he said, "Mrs Hirsh, I urgently need you here! Immediately!" He was almost screaming. The noise of the fire whirlpool was distorting the communications, and anything made of metal was melting.

Sarah asked, "But where is my son Simon?"

Fleming said, "It is for him that I need you here! Please, I will explain when you get here. Two of my agents will pick you up and bring you here. Please!" He hung up, not leaving time for Sarah to add another word.

As soon as Sarah put the phone down, the whole family inquired about Simon and his whereabouts. Sarah could not answer their questions, but she explained what Fleming had requested.

At that moment there was a knock at the door. Dan went and opened the door to reveal two FBI agents that Sarah knew. Sarah came and said to them, "I will be ready in one minute."

As she followed the two agents out a moment later, she asked, "Do you know anything about my son?"

One of the agents said, "Sorry, ma'am, but the chief will inform you."

Once they got outside, it grew incredibly hot. The sky seemed to be on fire. Sarah, sounding scared, asked, "Oh my G-d, oh my G-d, what … what … is this? What is happening?" She knew that her son had something to do with this. She had never seen the sky on fire.

In the meantime, Fleming was trying to get Simon to end this situation. "Pease, Simon, help us out," he said.

"My G-d, what can we do?" Tanner asked. He also screamed his lungs out trying to calm Simon, to no avail. The heat was unbearable, and the whirlpool of fire was a few miles wide now.

Tanner said, "Fleming, the same fires are all over the world. According to the newscasts, there have been over a billion deaths, and various cities are melting. It is the end of the world. These damned Iranians just blew it. They had their revolution, but Iran has ceased to exist, along with various other countries around the world. Giant tsunamis have drowned various coastal cities and islands. My G-d, it is Judgment Day. Why did this happen? It's partly our fault. Protecting Simon was too big of a task to manage."

At that moment Sarah arrived. She ran out of the car and straight to Fleming and Tanner, all in tears, her heart beating wildly. "Where is my son? Where is Simon?" she sobbed.

Fleming proceeded to explain what had happened as best he could.

Sarah said, "But you said that you would take care of him and that I had nothing to worry about. You lied to me." She was crying hysterically and pounding her fists against Fleming's chest. "My son, my son. I want my son."

Fleming pointed in Simon's direction. She did not wait and ran towards the column of fire around Simon. Fleming tried to hold her back, but in her desperation she didn't listen.

Suddenly something incredible happened. The fire separated and allowed Sarah to approach Simon. She shouted Simon's name. "Simon, Simon, my love, please answer me!" She kept screaming and repeating her plea, but Simon didn't seem to hear her.

Ten minutes passed, and finally Simon turned around and faced his mother. Fleming and Tanner hoped that Sarah could end this incredible situation.

In a very deep and unrecognisable voice Simon said, "Hi, Sarah, please do not come closer; you will burn."

Sarah said, "I am your mother. Please end all this. If you don't, this will be the end of the world, and that is against everything you stood for, my love."

"How can I?" Simon asked.

"But we all are going to die – your brother and sister, me, your grandparents. You cannot allow that."

Simon seemed to be reluctant and hesitating. Finally he said, "There is only one way."

"Yes, please tell me."

"Will you do anything to stop all this?"

"Yes, I will do anything."

"If you don't, there is no other way," Simon said.

"Yes, my love, I will do anything, please," she said.

"Here, listen," Simon said.

As he explained, she kept saying no and shaking her head from right to left. She began screaming, "No! No! No!" She ran back towards Fleming and Tanner crying and yelling, "No, no, no! I will not do that, no."

Fleming asked, "What happened? What did he say?"

"No, I will not do it," Sarah repeated over and over.

"Please, Sarah, explain," Tanner said. "The whole world is about to end. Over two billion people have been reported dead, vanished off the face of the earth. Please, Sarah."

Sarah was hysteric. Fleming held her face and tried to reason with her. Finally she said, still sobbing, "Simon said that there is one and only one way to stop everything. He has to be shot with a non-magnetic bullet."

Fleming said, "Maybe a gold bullet will do it. I will do it even though I love that child."

Sarah said, "That is not the worst part; I am the one that has to shoot that bullet, because I am the one that gave birth to him. That is the part that I will not and cannot do. He is my son, and he is my life. I will give my life for him at any given time."

Fleming said, "Time is running out, and we are going to die, all of us, even your family, your children. There will no world left for anyone. Over two billion people have vanished already. Please, Sarah, save us all."

"I will do it," Sarah said, her face pale as if she did not have a drop of blood left in her body.

Fleming did not rejoice at her acceptance to kill her own son. He hoped and prayed that he would never have to make this choice. Sarah was a wonderful human being with a heart bigger than the world.

Fleming called the lab and urgently requested a few bullets of pure gold for a .45 Magnum. The lab promised to have them to him within the hour. "No! You have thirty minutes and not one more," he said and gave the address where to bring the bullets.

Sarah felt dizzy and fainted. They rushed and got her a bottle of cold water. They sprinkled some of it on her face to wake her and then made her drink some.

Fleming said, "You gave us a scare. Please take a few minutes until the item gets here." He did not want to say *bullets*.

The thirty minutes seemed like an eternity. Finally a motorcycle arrived, and the rider asked, "Director Fleming?"

Fleming said, "That's me."

The young biker gave him a package and left. Fleming took the bullets out of his gun and put in the three gold bullets that he had just received. With a lot of tact, he handed it to Sarah and explained how to use it.

Sarah took the gun from him and was overcome with trembling. Tears flowed from her beautiful eyes that were blood red from crying. Tanner helped her to walk the first few steps. She then walked on her own but wasn't able to maintain a straight line. She was now on her way towards Simon. She was hoping and praying that this was just a nightmare and that she would wake up by the time she got to Simon.

Fleming and Tanner watched this terrifying picture unfold before them. It seemed that Simon was waiting for his mother to reach him. Everything around Simon was burned and on fire. The scene was unreal, like something from the worst horror movie.

Finally Sarah was about 10 feet from Simon and was crying hysterically. Finally she was able to mumble, "Please, my love, my life, don't make me do it. I will die right here with you. Please, please do not do this."

Simon said, "Sarah, I am David, and Simon is here with me. Do not worry about my corporeal envelope. My soul is safe, and I will go back to where I came from. Please do it to save our family. Time is going by fast, and people are dying by the millions. The bad ones are dying first. Please do it now! Now do it."

Sarah was shaking. She tried to do it without thinking, but it was too hard. Simon came closer, wrapped his hands around hers on the gun, and pressed the barrel against his chest. He begged her to pull the trigger, and a big sound resounded like thunder. The scene was eerie. Simon tumbled three steps backwards and seemed to fall to the ground in slow motion. Suddenly everything stopped. The whirlpool of fire ended as quickly as it had started. The sky slowly began clearing until it became normal.

Fleming and Tanner ran towards Sarah. It seemed like miles until they reached her. She fainted, and as she crumpled to the ground, she reached out towards Simon. He was lying there, inanimate, a very sad picture of a dead young child.

Both tough men began crying and tried to rescue Sarah. She had sacrificed her beloved son to save humanity. They took Sarah and made her come back to the sad reality and hurtful future that she had killed with her own hand her beloved five-year-old child.

Fleming held her against him, trying to calm her down, but he knew that words would not do it. They looked around at the scene of devastation. There were small dust piles everywhere, showing where bodies had disintegrated. Building was burned to the ground for miles around. People began coming out from their hiding places.

Fleming lifted Simon from the ground in his arms, and Tanner held Sarah against him to help her walk. They all mounted an F.B.I Black car that took Sarah and the children to the hotel parking garage where the rest of the family had taken cover during the whirlpool fire.

Sarah was afraid to look at Simon. She felt like a zombie, her shoulders slumped down. Suddenly a little hand grabbed hold of hers, and a little voice asked, "Mommy, what happened?"

All three jumped and looked at Simon, eyes wide open.

"Oh my G-d, what is this? A miracle!" Sarah cried her heart out, but this time her tears were of joy. She took Simon in her arms and kissed his face and his hands endlessly.

"Mommy, what happened?" Simon asked again. "Why are you crying?"

"You do not remember? Nothing?" Sarah asked. "What do you remember, my love?" Sarah had been revived; she couldn't contain her happiness.

Fleming said, "We are so happy that you are OK." He looked at Simon's chest and saw no bullet hole.

Simon asked, "Who are you? Do I know you?"

Sarah, Fleming, and Tanner looked at each other, and for a moment they were totally confused.

"David?" Sarah asked.

Simon asked, "Why are you calling me David?"

They all smiled, and Tanner said, "It is better this way. He will be able to live like a normal child." They all laughed.

Simon looked at his mother and winked. She was the only one that saw it.

The End

The S.E.G